# GLASS HEART

# GLASS HEART

## AMY GARVEY

An Imprint of HarperCollins*Publishers*

HarperTeen is an imprint of HarperCollins Publishers.

Glass Heart
Library of Congress Cataloging-in-Publication Data

Garvey, Amy, 1967–

Glass heart / Amy Garvey. — 1st ed.

p.     cm.

Summary: Wren Darby is struggling to keep her life in balance as she
juggles her blossoming relationship with Gabriel, shocking revelations about
her family's past, and the darker side of the powers that have been passed
down to her from her parents.

ISBN 978-0-06-199624-5

[1. Magic—Fiction.   2. Psychic ability—Fiction.   3. Horror stories.]
I. Title.

PZ7.G21172Whe 2012                               2011052410

[Fic]—dc23                                              CIP

                                                              AC

Typography by Torborg Davern

12   13   14   15   16     CG/RRDH     10  9  8  7  6  5  4  3  2  1

❖

First Edition

FOR SARA, WHO CAN IMAGINE
ANYTHING, EVEN WINGS

"Hearts will never be practical until they can be made unbreakable."—*The Wizard of Oz*

# CHAPTER ONE

I'M FLYING. SOARING, SWOOPING, DIZZY WITH power and the sharp bite of the December air on my cheeks.

The world is wide-open sky, cloudless and clear, and I can go anywhere.

Except, okay, I'm not really *flying*. More like skimming, feet hovering inches above the floor of the pedestrian tunnel that runs under the train station. It feels like flight, though. It feels *fantastic*.

Like I was meant to use the power inside me. To light up the dank cement walls with shimmering color that bleeds gold and silver and blue, washing them clean. A sort of holiday show, even if I'm the only one who can enjoy it, down here alone.

Except I'm not, I realize when I turn my head, my body following lazily in the air, a slow-motion hummingbird in a ratty winter jacket. A boy and a girl who look a few years older than me, probably college kids home on break, are standing at the southern mouth of the tunnel, and even though they're backlit I can see their expressions in the flickering reflection of my lights.

They're not shocked, though, or even scared. They look . . . delighted. As if they know exactly what I'm doing, and how.

That can't be right.

It's pure instinct to *push*. It just happens, a panicked rush of power spiraling out like aftershocks. The lights flicker crazily and die, I hit the ground with a distinct thud, and the boy stumbles backward.

But the girl grins. In the last shadow flare of light, her hair is the color of ice around a face that could have come from a vintage postcard. I know I've seen her before, even if I can't think of where right now.

I spin around and break into a run, pounding through the northern end of the tunnel and up the steps to the street, my bag banging clumsily at my side and my scarf flapping out behind me. I dash across the intersection just as the light is about to turn, and someone in a minivan leans on its horn.

I make it to the opposite corner and sag against the pale stone wall of the bank before I take a deep breath. The power is still crackling inside me, and the buzz of heat and energy licking through my veins feels so good, I close my eyes to let it rush through me a moment longer.

That doesn't change how stupid it was to do what I did, even in the train tunnel.

Then again, who would ever believe I had anything to do with it? I'm just a short teenage girl with freaky hair and fingerless gloves shivering on the sidewalk. When no one believes magic exists, it can be pretty easy to get away with it. It doesn't mean there aren't consequences, though. I know that better than anyone.

I should be more freaked out. Terrified that two randoms caught me doing something no one should ever see. Magic like mine isn't a spectator sport.

But right now the dizzying rush of spent power and adrenaline feels too sweet to ignore. Or to waste on worrying. So I lean against the cold wall like I have all the time in the world, waiting for the bright-hot glow of it to fade.

When I'm not vibrating with energy anymore, I push off the building and walk down Elm until I can turn the corner onto Quimby Street. I see Gabriel at the end of the block, standing on a ladder, a brown wool hat pulled down over his ears. He turns his head and spots me, the way he always seems to, and there it is, that breathtaking, happy *whoosh* inside me.

His whole face changes when he smiles. He's nearly six feet tall, all lines and angles, but when he looks at me that way? His mouth curves up so slowly, and his eyes get wider, darker, and everything that seems sharp about him on first glance softens.

I can remember the last time I was this happy, and that's what scares me. The last time I felt like this was in the early days with Danny, when everything was new and amazing, and the whole world had a bright smear of happiness on top.

Gabriel and I both know how that ended.

I thought the novelty of being with him would wear off after more than two months together—really together, no secrets or angry friends or dead boyfriend between us. That being with Gabriel would seem comfortable and familiar, maybe even a little boring. Instead, it's still a surprising rush, just as intense as using my power.

The difference is that the power inside me is pure heat, a buzzing, fierce vibration that shocks through me. It's always a little jarring at first, a surprising jolt.

Being with Gabriel isn't like that at all. It's a taste of the cleanest, sweetest water you can imagine, cool and pure and addictive, rushing in to fill every crack, soothe every smarting, rough place inside, but it never fills me up. Even now, I always want more.

"Hey there," he says when I'm standing beside the ladder looking up at him. In one hand he has a giant blue Christmas ornament with Superman's *S* emblazoned on the front, and he ruffles my hair with the other.

"Jeez, hold on," I warn him, ducking out of reach and pulling my earbuds out. "You're no good to me broken, DeMarnes."

He snorts and hangs the thing from the hook under the eaves in front of the shop window. It spins there lazily, glowing in the last bit of sun. "Oh yeah, that four-foot drop would be a killer," he says as he climbs down. His nose is cold when he bends in to kiss me, and I smile against his mouth. For a minute, we just stand there, foreheads together, his hands hooked in the pockets of my old blue peacoat, and I forget that it's four thirty on a weekday afternoon in the center of town, in the freezing December chill.

"You okay?" he says, looking at me closely.

"Totally fine." I pull back enough for him to see my smile. I know he can feel it, the leftover buzz of power shimmering around me, even if he doesn't look inside me anymore without permission. "What time do you get off?"

He wraps my loose scarf around my neck and brushes his thumb over my bottom lip. "Six, I think? But we're really slow today."

We walk into Verses, and the dry paper smell of the shop hits me when the door closes behind us. The walls are lined with shelves, and a huge, double-sided display looms in the center of the store, racks crowded with comic books. Batman glares at me from a faded poster as I follow Gabriel to the counter in the back.

"Ah, the other half arrives," Sheila says, looking up over her glasses at us. "You're late today, missy."

"I'm not here every day," I insist, and fight the blush heating my cheeks.

"No, not every day," Sheila agrees with a sweet smile. She's wearing an elf's hat over her straight black hair, and the bell on the tip jingles when she moves. "Just every day that Gabriel works."

I roll my eyes at her, but she just laughs and opens her book again, pushing her glasses up the bridge of her nose. On the cover, blood drips artfully from the title over a picture of a farm: *Blood Harvest.*

"That looks cheery," I say, and prop my elbows on

the counter as I scan the latest flyers and handouts Sheila always piles up for customers.

"What's cheerier than violent, ancient evil under the surface of unsuspecting small-town America?" She holds up her fist without looking away from the page, and I bump it and laugh. Sheila needs horror and sci-fi the way most of us need air, and Verses doesn't sell anything else but comic books and fantasy.

"Let's hope she never runs for mayor," Gabriel says, grinning at me from behind her, where he has his time sheet in hand. "You really need me anymore today?"

Sheila waves a hand absently. "Go forth, young lovers! But Saturday is a week before Christmas, so plan on being here all day. I'm hoping for desperate shoppers who can't get out to the mall."

"You're awesome," Gabriel says, and scribbles down the current time on his card. "See you Saturday."

He loops an arm over my shoulders as we leave. It's nearly dark already, and the wreaths hung from the street lamps are all lit. "Jingle Bell Rock" is playing through the speaker rigged outside the music store down the block, and a guy in a Santa suit is standing outside the card store, handing out candy canes. He yawns as we pass, and his fake beard slips down his chin.

Walking down the street with Gabriel like this is still

a little strange, same as sitting with him during lunch at school, or seeing his number flash on my phone when I'm with Darcia and Jess and not having to hide it. But I'm done with secrets after what happened with Danny.

Not the big one, of course, because there's just no good way to tell your friends you can make it rain in the cafeteria or change the color of your hair with a snap of your fingers. But Gabriel knows, and that makes such a huge difference in my life, it's still unreal. He knows more about me than Danny ever did, until the end, but he likes me anyway.

"What are you thinking?" Gabriel says, rubbing his knuckles gently across my head. Comfortable, as if I'm his to touch whenever and wherever, and I pull out of reach just a little bit.

If I let myself, I would push into his touch like a cat, but the thing about me and Gabriel is, I may have given up on secrets, but he hasn't. Sometimes it seems like everything I still don't know about him is the essence of that clear, sweet water, and that's why I can never get enough. Sometimes it seems like the only thing I really know about him is that he likes me.

But then Gabriel's got his own freak flag to fly, since being psychic isn't something most of the kids at school are going to put on their college applications. And while most of them might be pretty pumped if they thought I could magic up some beer or change the grades on their transcripts, not many of them would be thrilled to know Gabriel can see inside them if he wants to.

But that's not exactly the kind of thing you talk about walking down the street on a cold afternoon.

"I'm thinking that I have no idea what to get Mom for Christmas," I tell him as we turn the corner onto Elm. What I see just down the block almost stops me in my tracks. "And right now, wondering *what* the hell Robin is doing."

My sister is outside the pizza place, two of her friends standing behind her, and she's *flirting*. With a boy who's shuffling and blowing sun-bleached bangs out of his eyes, his hands jammed in his pockets. He's a good four inches taller than Robin is, and he looks like an eighth grader. Robin's only in sixth.

"He seems a little old for her," Gabriel says uncertainly, although he slows down and grabs my arm before I can take another step. "But they're just talking, right? You know, in public."

He might be right, but all I can think about is how my twelve-year-old sister is smiling at a *boy*.

I know what she'd say. The same thing she's been saying all fall, ever since her own powers started to emerge. That she's not a kid, that she's old enough, that I have to stop treating her like a baby.

It's amazing how little I care when the boy she's talking to looks like he could eat her for lunch and one of her friends for dessert. Plus, she's probably supposed to be at Mom's salon anyway or on her way there.

I'm really good at rationalization when I want to be.

"Hey, Robin," I call, shrugging off Gabriel's hand and starting toward her. "Funny to see you here."

In my head, this is supposed to convey that I'm her Big Sister, meaning Important and Scary and Not to Be Messed With, even though this boy she's talking to could probably eat me for lunch, too. Height is not exactly one of my gifts, and the scariest I ever look is either during a trig exam or when I wake up in the morning.

Robin is blushing so fiercely, I'm amazed her cheeks aren't actually giving off heat. One of her friends—I can never remember if her name is Nina or Mina—is squinting at me, eyes trained on my earrings. I've got four in my right ear, two silver hoops, a crescent moon, and a tiny pink cupcake. The kid's always fascinated with whatever I'm wearing, and stands in the doorway to my room when she's at our house like she's going to catch me performing a ritual sacrifice or tapping out secret messages to another planet. I have the feeling her L.L.Bean khakis and sweaters are her mom's doing, not hers.

"It's always funny to see your face," Robin says, pure bravado, and the boy snickers.

I bristle, and for a moment it's really tempting to smack him across the street on a bolt of energy made of pure overprotective sister rather than magic.

Not that it's easy to ignore the power inside me, gathering into an angry little cloud. It's frightening to consider what I could do to this kid with an intentional jolt of magic. Gabriel comes up behind me then, and I can almost feel the warning I know must be on the tip of his tongue.

"Mom's waiting for you at the salon," I say, tilting my head and fixing my best "you're in trouble now" glare on my little sister. "She seemed a little pissed off when I saw her."

It's a calculated risk, since I'm not sure if Robin is supposed to meet Mom there or not, but there's no way for her to know if I've actually been to the salon, either. She wavers—I can see it in the way she glances up Broad in the direction of Shear Magic, and in the nervous clench of her jaw. "Yeah, well, I was just going there. I'm not even late, jeez."

"Guess you'll have to tell her that, huh?" Uncon-cerned, no big deal, when we both know that if Mom's really mad, the consequences usually suck big-time. "Bye."

Gabriel waits until we're safely down the block, the sound of my sister's fury only distant chatter, to say carefully, "So . . . this is a new side of you."

"Shut up," I say, but I'm trying not to smile. He's right. Usually I'm yelling at Robin to get out of my room or to stop poking through my bag or to leave us alone when we're curled up on the sofa watching a movie.

But even though she's still mostly my incredibly irritating, nosy, *noisy* little sister, she is my little sister. I know it's not like I can hang around checking out every one of Robin's potential crushes, but it's weird to see her poking her toe into the big, bad world of boys. So far, her toes have been safely stashed in her soccer cleats.

And even if Robin is still pretty far from it, I'm not ready for her to realize how dangerous love can be.

For now, I slip my hand into Gabriel's as we head up Elm toward home. It's full dark already, and in another block we've left behind the stores downtown for blocks of old, sprawling houses. Christmas trees spill soft, sparkly light through the windows, and wreaths are hung on doors and lampposts. It's a little like walking into a snow globe before it's shaken, so perfectly Christmasy it's nauseating, until I spot the giant blow-up Santa in board shorts, holding a piña colada and waving from a porch roof a few houses down. I snicker as Gabriel and I walk without talking for a while, fingers twined together through our gloves.

He squeezes my hand. "Cole's going to help me with the stuff for chem lab. I'm pretty sure I'm going to blow something up."

"I don't think Mr. Pastor is up for explosions," I agree, and Gabriel bumps his hip against mine, laughing.

*Perfect,* I think. It's cold and it's dark and I have mounds of homework tonight, but this moment is perfect—balanced on the edge of too little and too much. It's almost scary how much I love it, how much I wish I could wrap it up and keep it, even if it's nothing more than the two of us walking home before dinner.

"Madame Hobart, now," he says thoughtfully. "I bet she'd be up for reenacting some of the revolution scenes from *Les,* uh, *Misérables.*"

He screws his eyes shut, stopping on the sidewalk in front of a huge brick house strung with white lights and fussy little designer wreaths.

"Right now?" I joke, but he looks funny, and suddenly I don't think he's kidding. "Gabriel? Are you okay?"

He shakes his head and grabs my hand again. "Just a headache," he says. "Came out of nowhere."

I bite my bottom lip and glance sideways at him as we start down the sidewalk again. "Maybe you should go home instead of coming over. I know you have homework to do later."

He makes a face, but he says, "Yeah. I'll throw some aspirin at it, maybe veg on the couch for a while."

It's nothing but a headache, I know that, but the fragile perfection of the moment before is gone. The hateful, skeptical part of me whispers that it wasn't going to last anyway.

I shut it out and hold Gabriel's hand tighter as I walk him home.

# CHAPTER TWO

LIGHTS ARE BURNING IN THE HOUSE WHEN I walk up to the porch, and inside it smells like a spice explosion.

"Hello?"

"I'm in here," my aunt Mari calls from the kitchen. "I was out of, well, everything, so I thought I'd raid your fridge and make you all dinner at the same time."

So much for privacy until Mom and Robin get home, not that I really mind. It's cool that Mari comes by the house so often these days. For years before she and Mom made up, I had to meet her downtown or at her apartment if I wanted to see her. I drop my backpack by the front door and shrug off my coat.

"What are you making?" I walk into the kitchen, where the counter looks like the crime scene after a vegetable massacre. I peek into one pot. Something a really funky shade of orange is bubbling and spitting, and I put the lid back quickly.

"It's a surprise," Mari says, squinting at the directions on a bag of rice.

I snag a soda out of the fridge and escape up to my room with my bag before she can draft me into helping.

It's tempting to crawl into bed and close my eyes. If I do, I'll imagine what Gabriel and I could have been doing if he had come home with me, but that seems a little pathetic. Like one step away from doodling his name on my notebook in sparkly pen and practice-kissing the back of my hand.

And I'm trying to be sensible about this. Or at least not completely crazy. But Gabriel is pretty crazy-worthy, if that makes sense.

He's beautiful, for one thing, although I know boys hate to be called that. I could look at him for hours, his soft, gray eyes and the long lines of his body, the birthmark I found on the right side of his neck, a dark fleck shaped like a crescent moon.

But it's not even how cute he is. It's stupid stuff, like

the way he bites his bottom lip when he's reading. And stretches his legs way out in front of him, ankles crossed, sunk back into the sofa when he's really concentrating on something he's watching on TV. The way he lets Mr. Purrfect climb onto his lap and sniff his T-shirt and knead his chest, even when he's trying not to sneeze.

I sit up and groan. This is even worse than doodling Gabriel's name in sparkly marker.

Homework is the logical distraction, but when I consider the joy of reading another chapter of *Les Misérables* or working on trig problems, I push my backpack away until later.

My phone beeps, and I grab it. *Saved by the text message,* I think as I flip it open.

It's Darcia. WROTE ANOTHER SONG!!!

I grin, and text back: CAN'T WAIT 2 HEAR IT.

Music is her life. Last weekend she told me she'd started writing a bunch of songs based on *Wuthering Heights*. I can't really imagine what they're going to sound like, especially since I think Catherine is a moron and Heathcliff is a complete asshole, but that's not really the point.

Dar knows who she is and what she wants to be. Jess isn't quite as specific, but I pretty much figure if she's not running the world at some point, she'll at least be running her own company.

And then there's me. The one thing I can do isn't even something I can discuss with most people. Like you're ever going to see that on some guidance counselor's career quiz: "Would you rather save a life or turn your ex into a frog? Would you rather stock shelves or wave a wand?"

The idea of a wand is pretty funny, though. Even Mom rolled her eyes when we read the first Harry Potter book, and back then we didn't talk about our magic. I grab a pencil off my desk and sketch a figure eight, brilliant dark glitter in the air.

Unless it's something complicated, like, say, raising someone from the dead, I don't even need words. I don't need anything but me, focusing the power inside, and it's one of the only times I feel completely right in my skin. Like I'm doing what I was meant to do, built to do, my thoughts flowing out and crystallizing in something tangible, something only I can create. And inside, every part of me comes to life, too, the usual low static buzz of power humming hot and strong instead.

I'm painting Gabriel's name on the bare wall by the window in dark, glowing purple when my bedroom door opens. I don't even have time to blink before Robin is poking my back. Hard, too, her finger digging in under my shoulder blade.

"What is your problem?" I flinch her hand away and sit up, turning to face her.

"*My* problem?" She's vibrating, a little live wire of fury. "My problem is *you*. How could you do that to me? Seth probably thinks I'm as big a freak as you are now."

"His name is Seth?" I make it sound as close to "dog shit" as I can. If she's going to be nasty, so am I.

"Yes," she hisses, hands on her hips and leaning in close. She's going for "bad girl," but her breath smells like Kool-Aid and she's wearing a daisy barrette, which sort of ruins the effect. "And he likes me, and he's awesome, and I don't need you to ruin it the way you ruin everything else."

Whoa. I blink at her for a second, because that's really low. I get that she doesn't want me interfering with her crush, but what else have I ever ruined for her?

"What does that mean?" I say when I manage to find my voice.

"Oh, like you don't know." She rolls her eyes and backs up, folding her arms over her chest as if she's holding in the jagged pieces of her anger so they won't explode and tear up the room. "We find out that Dad isn't gone, not really, but do I get to meet him? The dad I barely even remember, the one I've missed my whole life? No, because *you're* not ready."

Oh. I close my mouth and swallow. She's not wrong.

It was October when Mom admitted that she's still in touch with our dad, even though we haven't seen or heard from him since I was about seven. With an undead boyfriend stashed in my new boyfriend's bedroom at the time, I could barely feel the shrapnel of that particular bomb.

Those are weeks I don't like to remember.

Ever since then, my life has been as close to good as I could imagine it would ever be after Danny died. Mom and Aunt Mari started talking again, I patched up my friendship with Jess and Darcia, and I finally put Danny to rest.

And I met Gabriel.

My life isn't perfect—whose is when you have trigonometry and Bride of Frankenstein hair and you don't have your driver's license yet?—but it's so much better than I thought it could ever be last summer, after Danny's car accident. My dad is a big unknown, a question mark where the man who used to carry me around on his shoulders used to be, and I want so much for seeing him again to be perfect that I keep putting it off.

Too much happiness is usually too good to be true, at least in my experience.

But Robin doesn't understand any of that, and she doesn't know anything about what happened with Danny after he died. It's not fair to make her wait like this, and I know it, but I can't handle it yet. The last two times she asked, I faked being sick for a whole weekend and then bribed her with twenty bucks to give me a little more time.

She makes a low, disgusted noise and rolls her eyes while I sit there, frozen and silent, trying to find the right words. "Jeez, don't bother. You're so *selfish*, Wren."

She turns on her heel to leave when Mom appears in the doorway, frowning. "Dinner's ready, ladies."

"Oh, well, you better ask *Wren* if she's ready," Robin says, and pushes past Mom to pound down the stairs. The last echo of her anger hangs in the room, a crackling hiss that makes the hair on the back of my neck prickle.

"What did I miss?" Mom says. She walks into the room and bends over to pick up a pair of skinny black jeans and a couple of balled-up shirts, tossing them into the laundry basket.

"Preteen Melodrama Theater." I try to smile, like it's no big deal.

Mom leans against the wall, eyes narrowed. "Uh-huh. Go easy on her, Wren. You remember what being that age is like."

I do, and it was terrifying. Not just because boys were suddenly interesting in whole new ways, and I suddenly needed a bra. I had all this weird power running through me, and a lot of the time it was literally shooting out of my fingertips. Get me angry—or sad or frustrated or even stupidly happy—and I shattered glass or made flowers grow out of the spilled vacuum cleaner bag. Once I made the fireplace growl like the mouth of some fairy-tale dragon, and the cat was so terrified he climbed the living room curtains.

The same thing is happening to Robin now. The difference is she can talk to Mom about it, which was strictly off-limits when I was her age. And even though now I understand why, it still stings that I fumbled around blind for so long.

"Not my fault her baby hormones are spazzing," I say, and get up off the bed, tossing the pencil over my shoulder as I do. "What's for dinner?"

"Vegetable ragout and brown rice." When she catches a glimpse of the face I make, all she adds is, "Yeah, well. Go easy on Aunt Mari, too."

Dinner's not something I would ever willingly eat again, but it's mostly swallowable. What's really awful is the conversation.

It starts innocently enough, when Mari asks about the menu for Christmas Day. In one voice, Mom, Robin, and I all blurt out, "We'll cook!" Mari's cheeks heat up, but she doesn't question it. Instead, she asks about the rest of the plans for the day.

"What plans?" I shrug, waving my fork until I notice it's dripping burnt-orange ragout. "Christmas is for sleeping late, opening presents, and eating too much food. There, plan complete."

Robin glares at me, and I stick my tongue out. "What else do you want?"

Her mouth is half open when Mom cuts in. Her expression is frighteningly thoughtful. "I was thinking company, for once. We've spent a lot of holidays on our own. I think it would be nice to invite Gabriel and his sister here for the afternoon."

Mari lights up like someone plugged her in. "That's perfect! We can make cookies and have a fire and maybe even sing carols or something!"

"Did someone inject you with Hallmark?" I sputter. It's the first thing I can think of, but it's not even close to the point.

"Oh, come on." Aunt Mari waves her hand recklessly, as if this is completely natural and not, like, totally against the true order of the world. "It'll be fun. You said they're all alone, right? Do you really want them having lame Boston Market takeout in front of a Charlie Brown tree?"

I can't even form words at this point. My fork falls out of my hand onto my plate with a clatter, and the strange thing is that Robin's not even snickering.

"I'd love to meet Olivia," Mom says, and this time she's looking straight at me. "I like Gabriel very much, and it's clear you do, too. I met Danny's parents, Wren. Why not Gabriel's sister?"

There's no question now. The tone of her voice, calm and firm, all but spells out how very much this is a done deal. The best I can hope for is that the two of them have other plans. Maybe in another country.

"We don't have to sing," Mom adds with something that looks suspiciously like a smirk, and I glare at her. It's scary how easily she can read me sometimes.

"Well, I'm definitely making cookies," Aunt Mari announces, and gets up to clear her plate. It's not even satisfying to notice she didn't finish her meal, either. "Remember that year I made those gingersnaps, Rose? That was the same year I brought Kevin Tigerman to the house, and he almost broke his tooth on one of them."

Oh God. I bury my face in my hands.

"You know," Robin says out of nowhere, standing up as if she's making an announcement. Her voice is wobbling, though, and I sit back, frowning. "There's one thing that would make this big *family* day really perfect."

"Embarrassing party games? Baby pictures?" I snap, and Mom narrows her eyes.

"No, genius," Robin hisses at me. With her hand on one hip and her hair flipped over one shoulder, she looks like she's about to get up on the table with a protest sign any minute. "Dad."

These are the moments when you learn silence actually can be deafening. Underneath it, Robin's frustration is an angry, pounding heart, a drumbeat I can feel in my blood. Any minute, I'm sure, one of the windows will shatter or the pots will come banging off their hooks.

I probably should have seen it coming, after what she said to me upstairs. And I don't have a good reason to veto the idea, not off the top of my head. Why not add more fuel to the fire when the whole city's burned down anyway?

"I'm not sure that's a good idea," Mom says gently, and there's a shocker. When Robin opens her mouth again, Mom just holds up her hand and shakes her head. "It's been a long time, baby. A really long time. If you're going to see your dad again, I don't think you really want it to be in a roomful of people, do you? You and Wren should have some time alone with him first."

"I should have known," Robin says. She's trying not to cry, but it isn't working—her face is blotchy and red already, and her bottom lip is trembling. "It's all about Wren, right? Like *always*."

"Aw, honey, that's not true," Aunt Mari says, and reaches out to touch her shoulder.

Robin's too fast, so furious she snaps like a whip, flinching away from Mari's hand. "Yes, it is! Why couldn't we have Dad here instead of Wren's new boyfriend? How come no one thinks about what *I* want?"

She's gone before anyone can say another word, pounding up the stairs to her room. I wince when the door slams.

"We should really get the stairs carpeted," I say finally, and Mom narrows her eyes at me.

"Not funny, Wren." She gets up and carries plates to the counter while Aunt Mari sinks into Robin's abandoned chair. Even her curls suddenly look deflated.

"Do you want me to go up there?" she asks, and Mom shakes her head.

"Give her some time to cool off." She scrapes rice off her plate into the garbage and sets it in the sink. "She has a point, Wren. If you wanted to, we could certainly invite your dad here for Christmas instead, although I'm not sure what his answer would be."

I look up from the mess of mushy rice and vegetables on my own plate, startled. "Are you saying this is up to me?"

Mom's brow arches, and she shrugs. "I think I am. But it's either or, not neither, just so you know."

Great. I can choose whether to completely wreck my little sister and suffer through a day of mortifying family togetherness with my new boyfriend and hope my aunt doesn't accidentally poison him with her cooking. Or I can face up to meeting my dad again in less than a week.

For a second I close my eyes and summon up the fading scent of Dad's leather jacket, the image of the strong, square hands that used to tie my shoes, the sound of his low, surprised laugh when I tickled his nose with my hair.

I want that back. But it's too late now. I'm not a little kid anymore, and a lot of years have passed. I don't know who Sam Darby is, and after the last few months, I'm not sure I can stand it if he's not the man I remember.

Especially when the one thing I can't forget is that he's the man who walked away from us.

At ten o'clock I put down my trig book and groan, laying my head on the dining room table with a thunk.

When I lift it again, Mom is standing there, arms

folded, smiling. "Problem?"

"Tell me exactly how I'm going to use trigonometry in the future. Seriously."

"Nice try." She runs a hand over my head gently. "You should go up to bed soon, babe. It's getting late."

"Yeah." I sigh and scoop up my homework, which is scattered over most of the table at this point. It's easier to spread out down here in the dining room, and it's also farther away from Hurricane Robin, the preteen storm of angst. After dinner tonight, I was in no mood to even listen to her pouting through the wall between our bedrooms.

When I get upstairs, the door to my room is cracked a few inches, and I scowl. It drifts open if you don't click it just hard enough, which means someone other than me was in here at some point after I came up for my backpack.

Since there's no clean pile of laundry on my bed, I'm pretty sure that someone is Robin, aka the biggest snoop in Snoopville.

I don't see anything obviously out of place, and my spare cash is still in my top drawer, stuffed in an empty box of cough drops. Then again, my room is, as usual, such a mess, it would be hard to tell if someone had come in and trashed it.

I drop my books on my desk and glare through the wall in Robin's direction before settling on the bed with my phone.

Gabriel answers on the first ring. "Hey there."

"You weren't sleeping, were you?"

"Nah." I can picture him smiling, and my heart trips a half beat faster. "Just watching TV."

For a minute we don't say anything, connected only by the sounds of breathing, but it's nice. I'm pretty sure I want him and Olivia to come for Christmas—or more precisely that I'm not ready to have my dad here yet—but I'm not going to ask Gabriel now. Not yet. I want to sleep on it, at least.

"Did you finish your trig?" Gabriel finally asks, and I hear a muffled yawn trailing off the end the word.

I groan. "Mostly. I think it was designed to torture prisoners of war. I mean, what other use could it possibly have?"

Gabriel laughs. I love the sound of it, this low, soft ripple of sound. "Uh, I think civil engineers probably need it once in a while, Wren."

"Fine, be logical." But I'm smiling when I say it, and I know he can hear it.

I know if I asked him, he'd be able to tell me how much I'm missing him right now, how much I wish he was here, curled up next to me, instead of blocks away. And he wouldn't have to use his ESP to do it.

"You sound tired," he says.

"I am." I shrug and rub my eyes. "We should both go to bed soon."

"Yeah."

But it's a good twenty minutes before we hang up, talking about nothing and everything, and I wouldn't have it any other way.

# CHAPTER THREE

GABRIEL IS WAITING AT MY LOCKER IN THE morning, slouched against the dented metal door and talking to Jess. A couple months ago, I never would have believed it. What's startling is they actually like each other, too.

"Yeah, I don't know," Jess is saying when I get close enough to hear her in the early morning noise of the hallway. Her hair is scooped up in what I think of as her all-business ponytail, and even her sweater is a no-nonsense gray. "There's a slight Neanderthal vibe once in a while."

"From Gabriel?" I snort, and Gabriel lifts one slim

blond eyebrow. He's a little pale, and he looks tired. "He is to cavemen what I am to Amazons."

"How do you talk to boys you *don't* like?" Gabriel says, and ruffles my hair.

"Not Gabriel, you goof." Jess rolls her eyes, but she's blushing, too, and studying the front cover of her history notebook a little too intently. "Cal Gilford."

Cal Gilford? I twist the dial on my lock, trying to hide my surprise. Cal Gilford is the ultimate high school jock—big, broad, beefy. Definitely a blunt instrument on the football field and not exactly sharp anywhere else. At least not that I've ever noticed.

And while Jess may sometimes look like the ultimate blond cheerleader, she's really, really not.

"Don't say it," she warns when I finally turn around with my French book and shut my locker. "He's . . . cute, okay? And he's not as dumb as he looks."

"That's a glowing recommendation," Gabriel murmurs, and I bite my lip to keep from laughing.

"I mean it," Jess insists. Her cheeks are hot with color, but she's trying not to laugh, too. "He asked me to help him with his World Lit paper, and he's really kind of sweet."

"So . . . you're dating him?" I can hear how dubious I sound, but it's hard not to be. Jess doesn't date often, mostly because her standards are roughly Everest height, and when it comes to academics she's the kind of dedicated that gets you into the Ivy League. It doesn't leave a lot of time for boyfriends.

She bristles, and beside me Gabriel tries to disappear into my locker. Jess is intimidating when she's mad. When she's furious, she's terrifying, but she's not quite there yet. "Maybe. It's winter break in a week. I could use a little fun." Her mouth curls into a smirk, and she looks at me from beneath her lashes. "Especially yummy fun. I mean, even you have to admit he's decent eye candy."

I can feel Gabriel staring as they wait for me to answer. Like he has anything to worry about. Half the girls in school are homicidal that I got to him first, if only because he was someone new. "Sure," I tell Jess, summoning what I hope is a convincing smile. "Probably, um, mouth candy, too."

Jess's eyes widen but she snickers. "Classy, Wren." She gives me a mock salute before walking off to homeroom.

"Mouth candy?" Gabriel says as we head down the hall the other way. "Seriously?"

I elbow him in the ribs, not gently. "Shut up. I had to say something. And 'eye candy in a brute knuckle-dragging way' didn't seem very nice."

"Probably not," he agrees, and drapes his arm over my shoulders.

"How do you feel?" I ask as we walk into homeroom.

"I'm fine," he says as he slides into his seat. "Stop worrying."

Before I can say anything else, even to change the subject, Audrey Diehl comes in with Cleo Darnell, and I catch the tail end of their conversation.

". . . gone for three days. Scary, right?"

"I remember him," Cleo says thoughtfully. "He was sort of cute."

Audrey rolls her eyes and drops into the chair in front of Gabriel's. "He's *missing*, Cleo. I don't think his looks are really the issue here."

"I'm just saying," Cleo protests, and sniffs, wounded, as she digs in her bag.

For her lip gloss, I'm sure. In Cleo's life, there's no tragedy that can't be solved with the application of a little more Frozen Raspberry Glacée.

"Who's missing?" I ask Audrey.

"Adam Palicki." She shakes her head, and when she looks up at me, her eyes are troubled. "Remember him? His parents enrolled him in Saint Francis after eighth grade because they wanted him in smaller classes with more supervision or something. It's not like I really hang out with him anymore, but I've known him since kindergarten. It's weird."

I nod unhappily, even though I barely remember him. "What do you mean by missing, exactly?"

"As in not around, Wren," Audrey snaps before she takes a deep breath and gives me a tight, semi-apologetic smile. "Sorry. I mean, he walked out of the house Tuesday morning to go to school, and no one's seen him since. Or that's what they're saying, anyway."

"It's messed *up*," Cleo says, and if she thinks that brilliant observation is going to win her points with Audrey, she's wrong. Audrey may be the prototype of the popular girl destined to win prom queen, but she's not stupid, and Cleo, sadly, pretty much is. It's a good thing she's beautiful.

"Morning, ladies and gentlemen," Mr. Rokozny says as he walks in, letting his briefcase drop on his desk with a bang. "Let's get this show on the road, shall we?"

And that's the end of the conversation, at least for the time being. When I glance at Gabriel, he's only half listening, looking at his French notebook idly. He doesn't know Adam, after all—Gabriel and Olivia only moved here in October. Then Rokozny starts barking out the roll the way he does when he's in one of his fouler moods. I slide my foot across the aisle and toe at Gabriel's ankle until he looks at me, so I can smile at him.

He smiles back, and when Mr. Rokozny isn't looking, I reach over to hold his hand. Gabriel's smile turns into a grin, and it's so sweet I can nearly taste it.

★ ★ ★

The news about Adam is all over school by lunchtime, but it levels out at a low hum. No one's really hung out with him for more than two years, and aside from people in his neighborhood, like Audrey, no one's even seen him. Saint Francis is way across town, and most of the kids who go there are enrolled practically at birth. They tend to stick together in a big, uniformed crowd, and I guess Adam fit in well enough.

Gabriel's picking at a ham sandwich instead of eating it, and he doesn't object when I lay my head on his shoulder while Jess chatters mostly to herself about the pros and cons of letting Cal take her to the movies.

"By the time midterms are over, I'm going to be so brain-dead, I'd probably go out with him," Jess says, and jerks her head at the next table. Tiny little Duncan Miley, a freshman, is sitting by himself, scowling at his PSP. His faded Cthulu T-shirt is only a slight improvement over the World of Warcraft one he had on yesterday.

"He'd probably die of fright." I get the pink end of her tongue pointed at me for that before we all separate to head to our next class. Gabriel kisses me before Brian Sung snags him to walk to chemistry, and I realize I can still taste him when I slide into my seat in World Lit.

Darcia looks up, eyes wild and hair wilder, corkscrewing all over. "I'm going to fail this exam. I am *totally* going to fail this exam."

"Dar." I reach across the aisle and lay my hand on her arm. "The exam isn't until next week. We can study all weekend. You are not going to fail, I promise."

She ignores me, indignant. "Who writes a book about turning into a giant bug, Wren? I mean, come *on*."

She's not a straight-A student, but she's also not stupid. She just thinks she is, which sucks in ways that make me want to do horrible, vile things to whoever made her feel that way. And she's in the same boat I am—she's going to need both financial aid and scholarships, or it's the county community college all the way.

It doesn't help that her older sister scored a full ride to Rutgers. We don't talk about Davina much.

Darcia either missed the news about Adam or she's too stressed to care, which isn't like her. Not for the first time, I wish I could do more than sit her down and quiz her on themes and symbols, and suddenly I blink, Mrs. Duvall's voice a vague drone as she begins class. Who am I kidding? I could totally help Dar with this.

My power flares to life, and it's startling. I close my eyes for a minute, concentrating on taming it. What the hell am I thinking? I can't use magic on Darcia.

I mean, I *could*. I could do a lot of things, and most of them aren't anywhere near as taboo as bringing someone back from the dead. Dosing my best friend with magic is either brilliant or one of the sketchiest ideas ever.

When I finally hear Mrs. Duvall's voice, it's half amused and halfway to assigning detention. "Ms. Darby? *Wren Darby.* Contrary to popular opinion, this classroom is not the place for a nap."

I open my eyes and scramble upright, guilty and blushing. "Sorry. I was, um, thinking."

Someone snickers across the room, and I can see Darcia out of the corner of my eye, looking at me like I've completely sprained my brain.

"I hope you didn't hurt yourself. If you're ready?" Mrs. Duvall says, dry as sand.

I know from experience that the floor never conveniently opens up to swallow you, which makes wishing for it pretty useless. "I am."

But I miss most of the discussion on Gregor Samsa's identity anyway. Sometimes it seems like everyone has an identity but me. And the one thing that sets me apart— the one thing I can do well—is a power I can't even share with my best friends.

# CHAPTER FOUR

"YOU'VE BEEN WEIRD TODAY."

I glance up at Gabriel, startled. "Me? Are you kidding? You're the one dragging yourself around like you're in a coma."

He makes a face. "Thanks."

The diner is noisy and a little too warm, the windows streaked with fog. It's become our Friday night ritual, as long as I'm not working. For some reason, Gabriel always orders the meat loaf special with mashed potatoes and a huge house salad with Thousand Island dressing, like he secretly dreams about eating dinner in the fifties.

I balance on the edge of my seat to stretch forward

and bump my knee against his. "I'm sorry. I know you feel shitty."

"I'm *fine*. But you're . . . I don't know." He pushes lettuce around his plate, until it's drenched in creamy orange dressing. "Forget it."

I can't, because I know he's right. Even when he's not purposely poking around in my head, he picks up on a lot more than he mentions. My boyfriend, the human radio tower.

When it comes to Gabriel, I might as well be made of glass. He can see right through me all the time, good and bad, and when I'm feeling the most breakable, I hate it. But I don't feel like talking about my power now, or that I actually considered using it on Darcia for a minute. My power is just for me. For stupid things like writing Gabriel's name on my wall.

"It's messed up about that kid Adam," I say finally. It's not a lie, not really. Kids don't usually go missing here. Every once in a while someone gets pregnant, and a couple kids have wound up in rehab, and a few years ago Mikey O'Connor made a career out of getting arrested, but that's about it.

"Yeah." He pushes his plate away, half of his meal still uneaten. "Did you know him?"

"Not really." I break off a piece of my grilled cheese

and dip it in the cup of marinara on my plate. My mom knows Sheryl, our waitress, and Sheryl can always convince the guys in the kitchen to make me grilled Swiss on sourdough with sauce on the side. "I mean, I know who he is, but we weren't ever friends."

Gabriel dips one finger in my marinara and licks it off, shrugging.

"You want to get the check?" I ask him, brushing greasy crumbs off my hands and pushing my plate away. "Or is there room for pie?"

"There's always room for pie." He grins, and I smile when I feel his foot beneath the table, the toe of his sneaker gentle against my ankle. "You want to share?"

"Only if it's apple."

"God, you're so predictable," he says, but I catch the glimmer in his eye that means he knows exactly what I think about his usual dinner.

I'm about to kick him under the table when I see her across the diner, the girl from the tunnel. I shiver, frozen in my seat.

She's with another boy this time, as dark as she is light. He's slouched against the counter up front while they wait for a table, almost black hair hiding his eyes, a huge overcoat the color of charcoal falling in wrinkles of old wool below his knees.

He's chewing on a thumbnail like it's his mission in life, but she sees me, and even from all the way across the room, the weight of her gaze is a tangible thing. A touch, but not a heavy one—instead, it's sort of fond, fingers against the cheek of someone you love.

Gabriel is too busy flagging down Sheryl to notice. I grab my bag and start digging through it for my wallet, anything to look away from those pale blue eyes and the cloud of white hair around her face that looks like cotton candy.

She knows. She knows what I did, what I can do. I don't have to be psychic to recognize it for the truth. We're going to have to walk right by them to leave, too, and for a blinding moment I want to startle her, blow the two of them through the door with a thunderclap or a cloud of blue-gray smoke.

I want to show them what I can really do.

It's so tempting, all that energy sharp on my tongue. I drag my gaze up from my wallet, clutching sweaty, crumpled bills in one hand, and blink. Gabriel is squeezing the bridge of his nose like he's trying to get the whole thing to come off, and behind his hand I can see he's wincing.

Sheryl walks up to the table then, check in hand, and I don't bother to ask Gabriel before I say, "Can we get a slice of apple pie to go?"

By the time she's gone, the girl and the boy have been seated in the back room, on the other side of the wall. Gabriel hasn't looked at me yet, and worry uncoils in my stomach like a greasy rope.

I reach across the table to hold his hand until the pie comes, and this time he holds on tight.

"You totally don't have to come, you know. Seriously."

Gabriel sighs, and noses at my cheek until I turn my head far enough for him to kiss me again. "We're coming," he says against my lips. "But right now I think we could be doing something a lot more fun than talking about Christmas."

We're tangled on the couch at his apartment, and we didn't even pretend to put on a movie tonight, since we never end up watching them. Olivia tends bar downtown on Friday nights, so we always have the place to ourselves. My mother wasn't thrilled about it until I promised her I would keep my cell phone on and always answer it if she called.

I also reminded her that we'd already had the hugely embarrassing sex talk, when Danny and I were together.

"That was then," she'd said, words tart and heavy in the air. "This is now." I was just grateful she didn't insist on going over the particulars again.

I wonder what she would say if she knew it's one of the only things Gabriel and I haven't talked about.

Kissing is so much easier than talking. And usually a whole lot more fun.

The sofa isn't really big enough for the two of us, despite how short I am and how lanky Gabriel is, but neither one of us has ever suggested going into his room instead. I don't want to, not yet, and maybe Gabriel knows that. Maybe he just doesn't want to push. Either way, I'm content right here, tangled together warm and close, my hand on his chest and his arm around my back, his fingers in my hair.

"Are you sure Olivia won't mind? About Christmas?" I wince when he groans. I waited to ask him until we'd finished the last sticky crumbs of the pie, and I only brought it up because his headache seemed to back off as we walked home.

"I swear," he promises, and tugs lightly on a lock of my hair. "It's not like we had anything planned. And I wanted to see you on Christmas anyway."

"I know, it's just the whole family thing is so . . ." I don't even know how to finish that sentence. Not without saying things I don't want to admit out loud.

"Cool," Gabriel says distinctly, and the vibration of

his voice tickles my cheek. "It's not a big deal, Wren. I bet Olivia will melt all over it. We haven't had a family Christmas in a long time."

I know his mom died when he was pretty young but not much else about her. And I still don't know why Gabriel's dad is gone or where he is. I want to ask if they had any traditions, even if they were just dinner out somewhere or an afternoon at the movies. Three's not a big number, but it's still a family. For a long time, it's all I had with Mom and Robin.

But even without Gabriel's psychic gift, I can feel shutters banging closed in his head, the locks to every door turning sharply. Even his body is tense now, and I rub my palm in circles over his chest until he relaxes.

"Well then, I'm glad," I whisper, and stretch up to kiss him, licking the cinnamon of the apple pie on his lips.

"No singing, though," he says. "I draw the line at singing."

I laugh against his mouth, and he takes it in, smiling even as our mouths meet. I want to know so much more—the big stuff like where his dad is, how his mom died, and the stupid stuff, too. What his first-grade teacher was like, if he ever dreamed about being a fireman or a space cowboy when he was a little kid.

But he's kissing me, which makes it hard to think about anything else, or anything at all. I'm dizzy with the scent of him, spicy boy and worn, soft denim, and the faint taste of sugar and coffee on his tongue. I close my eyes and let go, until there's nothing left but all the places we're pressed together and the sound of our breathing, rougher and ragged now. Just another minute, I tell myself. Maybe two. Enough to pick apart and remember later, when I'm alone and wishing I had more.

And then it starts to change. I feel it in my blood, liquid gold sliding slow and hot through me, shimmering. When Gabriel takes my hand, pressing our palms together and twining our fingers, our heartbeats are right there, suddenly one, a sure, steady pulse echoing through our skin. It's hypnotic, perfect, seeping into every cell as if we're fused, and all the ways I can think to describe it are too much and too little. It's like a candy buzz, or the first dizzying swoop of beer in your stomach, the sensation of floating right before you fall asleep, the needling heat of a foot gone to sleep. All of it and none of it, but *good*. So good . . .

Gabriel wrenches his mouth away, creates space between us somehow, and blinks up at me, shuddering. "Wren. What . . . it was all . . . bright and hot and . . . like falling. Did you . . . feel that?"

It takes me a minute to remember how to breathe, to remember how to think and speak. I'm shivering, cold now that we're not pressed so tightly together, and whatever was running wild inside me is seeping away, nothing left but a pale shimmer of light.

"Yeah," I whisper, and sit up, pushing my hands through my hair and taking a deep breath. "I mean, something like that. It was my power, I think."

He sits up, too, blue-gray eyes dark and hot, and runs a hand across his forehead like it hurts again. "What do you mean?"

"I don't know, okay?" I need some water, some cold air, a minute to think. I don't know what would have happened if he hadn't stopped. I know I wasn't even considering it. It was delicious, even if it didn't exactly feel real. It was hard to care about how far off our usual map we were in the moment, and that scares me.

Gabriel follows me into the kitchen, and I fill glasses with water for both of us. He leaves his on the counter while I drain mine, gulping the last bit and wiping my mouth with the back of my hand.

"You okay?" His voice is low, and he's still flushed. I nod, and for a minute we just stand there, looking anywhere but at each other. The kitchen floor is ancient red-brick linoleum, and I trace the outline of one rectangle with my socked toes.

I slept with Danny, after we'd been together for months. I didn't regret it then, and I don't now. It still feels right that we gave each other that, because he'd never slept with anyone, either.

Going slow with Gabriel isn't really about not wanting to sleep with him, though. It's about what happened after, with Danny. How much closer I felt to him, how many more secrets we shared, this new private language we had together.

But now, with Gabriel, there's so much I still don't know. So much he still doesn't say out loud. We have to speak one language together before we can learn another one.

Gabriel clears his throat, and for a second I want more than anything to reach and brush away the pale sheaf of hair falling over his forehead as he studies his feet. But he's leaning against the fridge, all harsh angles, like he's about to fold himself away. Just because he knows what I can do doesn't mean it doesn't freak him out sometimes. "So, nothing like that ever . . . ?"

"No," I rush to say, because we don't talk about Danny, not anymore. "I mean, not like that. Once in a while it felt sort of . . . floaty, but that was all."

When he lifts his head, the brief flash of heat in his eyes looks a lot like victory. It's one more reminder of the dozens of things I still don't know about him, like whether or not he's ever had a girlfriend, and who she was, what she was like. But now is not the time to ask. Not with Gabriel looking at me like that, and not with that warm, liquid-gold sensation still echoing faintly in my pulse.

"Do you . . . want to stop?" Gabriel says, and he sounds so unsure and so hopeful at the same time, I want to scream.

But I'm not four, so I take a deep breath. "I don't know. I mean, I . . . no, not really. It's just that I thought I had it under control, but it's all tied into my emotions and I . . ."

Another sentence I don't know how to end. Except that I actually do, I just can't say it out loud, not yet. *I love you.*

He folds his arms over his chest, holding in things he doesn't want me to see, or maybe things he wants to believe. But his voice is as low and gentle as ever, and I wish I could hold on to that, wrap the sound around me, and snuggle in. "Can't your mom help?"

"It's not Hogwarts, Gabriel." And there, I've ruined the moment already. He scowls at me, and I reconsider the futility of wishing the floor would open up and swallow me.

"I'm sorry." I take a step closer and pick at a stray

49

thread on the cuff of his shirt. "It's just that it doesn't seem fair. Not right now. Robin needs Mom, too, and she's already so busy. The salon is crazy this time of year."

"I know," Gabriel says, and moves away, taking his shirt with him. The stray thread flutters along with it, as helpless and unsteady as I feel, and I watch as he shudders out a breath. "I'm just talking about asking her a simple question."

"But it's not simple!" I sink back against the counter, and then slide to the floor, wrapping my arms around my knees. "It's finally out in the open, yeah, but it's not like our house suddenly turned into Magic Central. It was never like that, really. Mom and Aunt Mari and Gram didn't hide it when they used their power, but it wasn't an everyday thing, either. It was . . . something special." I close my eyes, letting the memories swim up, pale and faded before they resolve into sharper pictures.

The glimmering, dancing lights on my bedroom ceiling. Mom and Gram making a birthday cake, swirling frosting up and down the sides with the flick of a finger. Mom and Dad curled in the swing on the front porch in the dark, each swoop forward trailing soft jet streams of color behind it.

Gabriel sinks down beside me, winding an arm

around my shoulders and resting his chin on my head. "But isn't that a good reason to ask your mom how to control it? Or what it means if you can't?"

It sounds logical enough, but the whole thing is still more complicated than he understands.

I'm pretty sure I can do things that Mom can't. Not just things that she *wouldn't* do, but stuff that her power couldn't accomplish on its own, not without some serious spell work behind it.

I could be wrong. I am, a lot. But even though I know that my memories of Gram's power are limited, I've never seen Aunt Mari do anything like I can do with just a thought, either.

I close my eyes again, burying my face against Gabriel's chest. He's warm, solid, and I burrow in hard, pressing my nose to the worn cotton of his shirt. Behind my closed lids, a frail, white-paper bird flaps to life.

And a boy as pale and still as marble watches me in the musty dark of a garage loft.

I know what it feels like when Gabriel pokes inside my head. Vague pressure that's not really pain, the sharp light of day visible through a slightly open door. I pull away, even though he grabs my arm to keep me beside him. "Cut it out. You know I hate that."

He scratches his head roughly and lets go of my arm

to stand up. "Yeah, well, sometimes I can't control that, either."

For a minute we simply look at each other, and I wish I could read all the emotions I can see in his eyes as easily as he can read me, whether he's trying to or not.

He means too much to me already. The way he scratches his head when he's frustrated, the way he slouches just a little when we're walking together so the height difference between us isn't so obvious, the low hum in his throat when we've been kissing for a while. Tiny, insignificant things that don't come close to the way he trusts me, or the way he listens to me, but put it all together and just the sight of him makes my heart ache with how much I want to keep this. How much I want to keep *him*.

There's so much I don't know about Gabriel, but Danny leaked pieces of himself like someone had poked a hole in him. Not a day went by when I didn't hear how he felt about this movie or that band, and I can still make lists of not only his favorite foods and books and people but the things that made him who he was—the things he felt, in his bones and blood, about everything.

"I should probably go," I say, pushing to my feet and walking into the living room, where my boots are tossed in a pile on the floor with my coat and bag.

"Wren." Gabriel sits down on the sofa where I'm putting on my shoes. His cheeks have lost that hectic flush. "I'm sorry. Really. You can stay, we don't have to—"

"I know." I force my mouth into a smile. "But I think I want to, and . . . I don't trust myself right now. I'll come by the store tomorrow, okay?"

I don't kiss him good-bye when I leave.

# CHAPTER FIVE

"MY BRAIN'S GOING TO BE COMPLETELY broken by the time we get to Christmas break," Darcia says. Her notes and textbooks are spread around her on Jess's dining room table. It looks like a library heaved up its lunch. A stray pink Post-it Note is stuck to her sleeve, and her hair is twisted up on top of her head with two pencils.

"Breathe," Jess says absently, and flips a page in her chem book. "Cal called again last night."

Dar groans and picks up her copy of *The Metamorphosis*, ignoring her.

"And?" I say when Jess doesn't elaborate. Behind her

notebook, Dar scowls at me, and I shrug. Jess doesn't freak about exams, but she does sort of freak about boys. If you can call overthinking the possibility of one date freaking, that is.

"It was . . . nice." A satisfied little smile tugs at her mouth. "He's nice. Nicer than I thought anyway. Which is an excellent example of not judging a boy by his very footbally cover."

I raise an eyebrow. "Footbally?"

Jess waves this off carelessly. "You know what I mean. So I think I'm going to go for it. Almost definitely."

"*Meanwhile*," Dar says with a distinct edge to her voice, "I'll be grounded because I've failed all my exams, but you have fun. Be sure to tell me *all* about it."

Jess blinks, and even I sit up a little straighter. It's not that Darcia doesn't have a temper, but it usually takes something like dynamite and a four-alarm fire to set it off.

"I'm sensing a little sarcasm there, sweetie," Jess says in the perfectly calm, frightening voice I hate.

"Oh, do you *think*?" Dar answers before I can get a word out.

Jess's jaw is tight, but I can see it quiver. "What the hell crawled up your ass and died?"

"Hey, come on, this is stupid." I stand up as if I'm going

to have to physically break them up. I can't remember the last time Jess and Dar fought. Well, with me, sure, but not with each other.

"It's not stupid." Jess pushes her books out of the way and grabs her bottle of water. "I want to know what she has to say."

For a second, I'm sure Darcia is going to open up and explode, spraying angry words all over both of us. The air in the room suddenly feels too thick, oppressive, and Jess's golden retriever, Lass, whines from beneath the table.

Out of nowhere, I'm flooded with the memory of shouting, "Stop!" at Danny, and watching him crumple to the ground, strings cut and nothing more than a lifeless collection of bones in the grass. I shudder and turn around, digging into my bag.

I can't do that here, now, but I can do this. When I turn around again, my phone in my hands, Darcia's eyes are blazing darker than I've ever seen them. Jess is waiting for whatever Dar is about to say, fingers too tight around her water bottle, but I knew neither of them could ignore me.

"What the hell are you doing?"

I snap a picture, catching the angry set of Jess's jaw and the stray blond hair that she'll tuck behind her ear any minute now. "Taking pictures of my best friends acting like assholes."

"Hey," Dar starts, and I turn to her. The shutter clicks before she can close her mouth, and she blinks.

"Oh, that's a keeper," I say, looking at the screen. "Totally a Facebook moment."

"Don't you dare," Dar warns me, but she's trying not to smile now, and Jess actually snickers.

"Are we done now?" I set the phone down on the table. "Seriously, guys, it's exam week, not war. Get a grip."

"I wish I could," Darcia sighs. Her shoulders sag and she crosses her arms on the pile of books before laying her head on them. "All I keep thinking about is college applications and grades and scholarships and my sister coming home next week, and I just want to scream."

"As long as you don't scream at me, I'm cool with it," Jess says. She reaches across the table and pulls one of Dar's curls. "Come on. I think it's time to re-caffeinate."

I have to pull Dar to her feet, but we follow Jess into the kitchen, where she pulls three cans of diet soda out of a carton in the fridge. "I think I want a smoke, too," she says once she's cracked her can with a fizzy pop.

We troop outside through the kitchen door, and the dry brown grass is brittle underfoot. "Coats would have been smart," Dar says as we huddle together on the splintered wood bench behind the garage.

"Don't be a wuss." Jess reaches under the bench, where her pack of Marlboro Lights is stashed. When she lights up, she exhales a stream directly at Dar, who sticks out her tongue.

"I still need to get Gabriel something for Christmas," I say, scuffing the toe of my boot in the dirt. "I'm drawing a total blank."

It's really the least of my problems, when I factor in my trigonometry exam, which I *am* in danger of failing, Robin's continuing sulk, and whatever the hell happened between Gabriel and me last night, but it doesn't seem like it. I want to give him something awesome, something special, and I don't have any idea what that could be.

"A book?" Dar suggests, sticking her hands between her thighs, and huddling closer to me. It can't be more than thirty out here, and the air smells like snow, thick and damp.

I roll my eyes. "He works in a bookstore."

"How about a watch?" Jess asks, blowing a bluish stream of smoke in the opposite direction.

Dar and I exchange a look. Sometimes Jess forgets that the rest of us don't live on Planet Bling with her, not that she ever makes a big deal of how much money her family has. "I can afford roughly whatever comes in a box of Cracker Jack," I tell her. "I don't think anybody wants the kind of watch I can buy."

Dar bites back a laugh and reaches over to tangle our fingers together. Her hand is dry and cool. "What about burning him a CD?"

"Ugh. The mix solution." I sigh, and blow a plume of steam into the frigid air. "So completely lame."

"God, are you done?" Dar asks Jess. She's shivering beside me, and the pencils in her hair wobble. "My brain is now frozen, and I really want that soda, but I'm afraid my tongue's going to stick to it."

"You two would never make it as POWs," Jess says. She stubs out her cigarette, and we troop back inside. The kitchen is gloriously warm, but I'd still rather have a huge mug of hot coffee or tea than the cold soda.

"At least now I'm too cold to realize everything I don't understand about Kafka," Dar says with a groan.

"Come on." I grab her hand and lead her back to the cluttered dining room table. "I'll explain it again."

An hour later, Jess is reciting chemical elements under her breath, and Dar has moved on to irregular Spanish verbs. I'm still stuck on trig, even though most of my brain is elsewhere.

It's quiet aside from the bare branch that sometimes scrapes at the window, and Lass occasionally snoring under the table. Dar has her iPod on and a new pencil anchoring the crazy knot of her hair, and I'm getting sleepy. Trigonometry wouldn't be the most exciting subject in the world even if I understood it.

As I slouch in my chair, staring at my open notebook, I'm trying not to think about Gabriel. At least not about what happened last night.

I close my eyes, picturing it so perfectly, I can almost feel it again. The flush of heat, and beneath it that distant thrum of power, beating steady as a heart in my blood, in Gabriel's blood . . .

Nothing that feels that good is usually good for you.

"Hey, no sleeping on the job," Jess barks, and I jolt back to the present to find her watching me, one eyebrow cocked. "I find that study by osmosis doesn't work very well," she adds, and picks up her soda to drain the last few sips.

"Don't knock it till you've tried it." My voice is as wobbly as I feel just remembering last night.

"Damn, I should have gotten a picture of that," Jess says. "I could have Photoshopped in some drool."

"That's it!" I sit up so suddenly, I almost knock over my soda can.

"That's what?"

"Sorry." My face is hot, and my pulse kicks hard. "I know what I can give Gabriel for Christmas."

Jess scrunches up her face. "Your drool?"

I roll my eyes. "It's criminal that you're not on Comedy Central already, you know."

She rolls her eyes right back. "Fine, don't tell me."

Darcia takes out her earbuds. "What are you talking about? And so loudly."

"I figured out Gabriel's Christmas gift." I stuff my notebooks into my bag as quickly as I can.

"Oh! Cool. Wait, what is it?" she says. One cheek is a warm pink where she'd propped it on her hand, and she sounds half awake.

"Pictures," I say, and Jess looks up from her notes. "Places we've been, stuff like that."

For a second, in the dog-panting silence, I want to take it back. It's probably dumb, a cheesy do-it-yourself nightmare that he'll laugh at, and any minute Jess is going to say . . .

"That's perfect." She sits up straighter, tucking her hair behind her ears, all business now. "You take awesome pictures. Or . . . you know, you did there for a while."

I did all the time, before Danny died. A camera is a great way to put some distance between yourself and the world, and I liked being behind the lens. No one pays attention to you back there, at least after they forget you're clicking the shutter. I have a whole file on the laptop of pictures I took of Danny and his friends, of Jess and Dar and my family.

I pick up my jacket and shrug it on, not looking at Jess when I say, "It's not . . . lame?"

Her disgusted sigh is all the answer I need, although Dar chimes in with, "I think it's awesome."

"I'm going to go take some now." I shoulder my bag, biting my lip nervously. "This could be really good. I hope."

"It will be," Jess promises. She's smiling, feet tucked up on her chair and her arms wrapped around her legs. "Of course, I'm pretty sure he'd love it if you gave him, like, a ball of hair, you know."

"Oh my God, you're gross," Dar says to that. She looks forlorn, moored in her sea of paper. "Call me later? Dad's freaking about Adam's disappearance, so I'm pretty sure I'm stuck at home tonight."

"I will." I stick my phone in my bag and wave to Jess after I put my coat on. "I'll be around if you want to talk about Cal."

"We'll see," she says, and runs her hands through her hair absently as she stretches in her chair. "He's supposed to call again tonight, so he's got another chance to impress me."

"Lucky him." I pet Lass's head when she gets up to follow me. "You stay, girl."

Jess and Dar are already focused on their books again when I open the front door, and it's hard not to run, now that I've got the idea in my head. I can think of a dozen places that mean something to both of us, but I need to get to them before the light dies.

And if my camera isn't where I think it is, buried in the bottom of my desk drawer at home, I'm going to have to hope Gabriel really likes Cracker Jack.

In the papery winter light, I take pictures of the cornerstone of the high school in shadow, the splintered wood steps to the porch of Gabriel's house, and the bare branches of the huge maple on Forest Avenue where Gabriel dragged me all those months ago, to tell him about Danny. None of the shots are really what I would call romantic, but I work on each one, examining angles and shadows to make them interesting.

I hope they are anyway. I won't be able to frame them all, but I can mount them on heavy paper. I make my way downtown as the light is truly dying, pale white sky smudged gray at the edges, because I want to get shots of

Bliss and the bookstore, too.

I shrug down into my coat as I walk, and wind my scarf tighter around my neck. It's even colder now, and it's really beginning to smell like snow. The air is heavy, as if it's full of secrets, and I'm glad I grabbed a hat before I left my house. Olivia was home when I stopped there to take my first pictures, and she made me a mug of instant hot chocolate while I rooted around in Gabriel's closet for a pair of his shoes.

"What exactly are you going to do with those?" she'd asked idly, leaning in the doorway to his room, her own mug cradled in her hands.

"Um, take a picture of them." I gave her a hopeful "that's not weird, right?" smile. When I explained that I was going to take off my Docs and line the two pairs up side by side on the porch steps, she got it.

"That's pretty cool." She licked chocolate off her top lip. She looked half awake; when she was bartending on Friday nights, she got home long after midnight. "Are you doing color or black and white?"

"Black and white," I said, straightening up after I finally found Gabriel's faded blue Converse low-tops under his bed.

"I can't wait to see them." She smiled before wandering away, and I ran downstairs to set up my shot.

I didn't have the nerve to tell her she might see the pictures sooner than she thought, since I doubted Gabriel had had a chance yet to tell her about my mom's invitation to Christmas dinner.

I'm not too worried about her coming for Christmas, since she's pretty much the coolest older sister I've ever met, but the idea still makes my stomach roll over unhappily. Olivia is the only family Gabriel has, and if she isn't happy with me—and my weird little family of magical women—I know it will hurt him.

But I'm not going to think about that now. I still have pictures to take and print and mount, and an actual boyfriend to face later when he gets off work. My plan is to meet him outside the shop when he gets off, all casual "surprise!" But every time I think about him, the memory of last night pushes through, hot and urgent. I have no idea what will happen the next time we're kissing, and I still don't understand what happened last night.

For once, "playing with fire" doesn't sound like a lame cliché.

The next stop is going to be Bliss, where I am craving a latte as big as my head. I definitely don't want Gabriel to see me if he's in the front of the bookstore, so I decide to cut through the alley to come around from behind it. But the minute I look across the street at the café, I freeze.

The girl and the boy from the diner last night are just coming out, holding tall paper cups with the Bliss logo on them. The girl turns her head and spots me just as I'm about to back up into the alley, and her mouth stretches into a dangerous grin. This time the boy stares.

I feel like prey.

But I can't just stand there like a space case, and I can't turn and run again, either. I have too much pride for that. No matter what, they're just kids. Who would they even tell?

My feet start moving before I actually decide to take another step, but by then they're only five feet away.

"I was hoping I'd see you again, tiny barista," the girl says, and it clicks.

She comes into Bliss, usually in the evenings, and she always orders a triple espresso that she doctors with loads of sugar.

"I'm not tiny," is the first thing that comes out of my mouth, even though each of them has a good couple inches on me.

The boy tilts his head, smiling, and laughs. "You're totally wee. But it suits you."

He's decked out in the long wool coat again, with a Harry Potter–striped scarf wound loose around his neck. I want to ask him how the hell he thinks he knows anything about me, but as I open my mouth the girl reaches out to flick the collar of my jacket. Her nails are a deep, shimmery royal blue, like disco Disney, and longer than most girls wear them anymore.

"Don't mind him," she says, stepping between us and lowering the wattage of her grin to a more comfortable glow. "He was born with foot-in-mouth disease. It's tragic."

I stare at her, because it's hard not to. She looks like she just landed on Earth from another world, somewhere part Wonderland and part space opera. Her cloud of hair is so platinum it's colorless, but her eyes are a bright Christmas green, and her mouth is a blaring fire-engine red.

"I'm Fiona," she says, and holds her hand out. "I don't think I've ever properly blah blah yadda."

I blink, and my hand is reaching up to take hers without any conscious direction from my brain. "I'm . . . Wren."

The sound she makes isn't quite a laugh, but it's delighted. Behind her, the boy sticks his hand up, a half-mast wave. "I'm Bay."

"Bay?"

"Joseph Arthur Bayliss," Fiona stage-whispers. "His initials spell 'jab.'"

"Bay," he repeats, but he doesn't really sound pissed

off. "What's up, Wren? I heard about you."

This is it. The moment, the one I've been dreading ever since Fiona saw me in that tunnel. I wonder what happened to the boy she was with that day. He knows about me, too, or at least whatever Fiona thinks she's figured out about me and thought was interesting enough to tell Bay.

"We should talk," she says, and her voice sounds like silk in the frigid air.

"I don't have anything to say," I manage, and take a step around her instead of back. I head down the sidewalk, even though I know I can't stop at Bliss now and keep walking past it through the alley on Elm, which will cut through to Main. I can hear them following. "I don't even know you."

"But I know something about you." It's light, singsong, as she follows behind me, Bay right beside her.

I stop next to a parked truck behind the delivery doors to the dry cleaner's. Bay is staring at me, head still tilted to one side. I don't look away when I say, "Maybe you think you do." My voice doesn't even shake.

"Sweetie, you were a good eight inches off the ground." Fiona is suddenly much closer, her breath warm in the cold air. "You *know* I know, and it's cool! It's *awesome*, is what it is. We love a new playmate."

Bay hasn't even blinked, and I can't drag my gaze away. His eyes are so dark, they're as colorless as her hair, and I wonder if they're contacts. He's some weird combination of prep and Goth I'm not sure I've seen before, and it's almost funny.

"No pressure," Bay says finally, and I nearly jump, he's been so still until now. "But if you ever want to talk about what you can do, just let us know."

I put all of my bite into my words. "Do you hear me asking for your number?"

Bay smiles, slow and wise, and Fiona slips her arm through his as she tugs him away, calling over her shoulder, "It's already in your phone."

# CHAPTER SIX

MOM'S IN THE KITCHEN WHEN I WALK INTO the house twenty minutes later. I wound up heading home when I was trying to shake off my two new "friends," and suddenly I was too confused and off balance to turn around and face Gabriel. I'd been so worried about seeing Fiona again, and now she just seems like a harmless, flamboyant fairy with a bored poser boyfriend. I'm as mad at myself as I am at them, and I'm going to have to go back to get pictures of Bliss another day.

Mom's somewhere between putting groceries away and laying out ingredients, although it doesn't look like they're going to add up to dinner.

"Hey, kiddo. I thought you'd be off with Gabriel somewhere."

When I slide my arms around her waist and lay my cheek on her shoulder, I can feel the vague vibration of her laugh. "Glad to see you, too, sweetie. What's up?"

I twist my head to look up at her. "Can't a girl want a hug for no reason?"

"Sure. You just usually don't." She strokes my hair for a minute, her fingers catching in the coarse waves. "Wow, it's cold out there. Get your coat off and help me with this?"

I step back and carry my coat out to the rack in the front hall, peeling off my gloves and scarf, too. I wish it were as easy to shed the hard little knot of guilt wedged up under my ribs at what Gabriel must think of me not showing up.

Mom is humming something under her breath as she turns the knob on the oven to preheat it, and I start collecting the assortment of brown-paper grocery bags and folding them up to put away.

"What are you making?"

"Desi said she would close up the shop tonight," Mom explains, putting a new bunch of bananas in their bowl on the kitchen table. "She said, and I quote, that I looked ready to do violent murder, so I decided to come home and start on some cookies for next week."

I blink, speechless. Every day gets more like Dickens around here lately, and it's actually sort of nice. Before, when it was just me and Robin and Mom, cookies were usually a last-minute Christmas Eve thing, and sometimes just a ready-bake roll of dough from the supermarket. "Seriously?" I blurt out before I think twice, and Mom lifts an eyebrow.

"Yes," she says tartly, but she's smiling, too. "Once upon a time there was a more domestic me, for your information. And I'm trying to . . . well, get reacquainted with her."

"You go, Martha." I duck when she throws a roll of paper towels at me, and my elbow knocks into a bowl of eggs set at the edge of the counter. It's pure instinct—I blink again, the image of a ball flashing behind my closed lids, and as the eggs fall they round out, white and shiny, and bounce off the floor and against the cabinets. The glass bowl bonks down beside my feet, thick clear rubber, and spins drunkenly to a stop while Mom and I watch the eggs roll in slowing arcs.

Her mouth is open when I glance at her, and my cheeks heat with something that feels weirdly like pride.

"You amaze me sometimes," she says softly, and

reaches down to pick up the bowl carefully, as if it's some crazed wild animal.

I kneel to start picking up the eggs, which are already stretching back into ovals, pointed ends and round bottoms intact. "Is that . . . good?"

She doesn't answer for a minute, standing at the counter and watching the bowl gradually lose its rubbery coat. When it's done, she runs a finger along the rim, tracing the shape of it.

"I don't know," she says finally, and turns around to look at me. "You can do things I could never do at your age, and some things I'm not sure I could do now. Not off the top of my head like that, anyway. It's a little . . . startling."

I don't know if I'm supposed to apologize for that, so instead I carefully put the eggs back in the bowl.

Before I can think of what to say, Mom adds, "I was almost sixteen before my powers really showed up." She shakes her head, her eyes focused on something faraway. "Mari, too. I guess we didn't think about—"

She breaks off that thought so quickly, I can practically hear it snap. I don't know who she means by "we" and I really want to, but Mom's already turned around, doing a good impersonation of the woman she was a few months ago, the one who wouldn't talk about the magic.

I push the bowl away from the edge of the counter and sit at the kitchen table. I hate it when she does this, especially when I'm not ready to let the subject go. I hope if I keep my questions more general she won't turtle up completely. "Where did it start, do you know?"

She glances over her shoulder, one finger stuck on the page in the cookbook propped against the sugar canister. "Where did what start?"

I shrug. "What we can do. It had to start somewhere, right? And why is it only women?"

She's so still, poised over the cookbook, I'm afraid she's going to do the whole "turn this car around" bit that parents are so good at, but after a second she says, "I don't know, now that you ask. It's not just women, though." The last part is thrown off like an afterthought, even if it's the most interesting tidbit to me right now.

It means Bay could actually have powers, too, although he didn't show any sign of them. Come to think of it, Fiona didn't, either, unless I really do find her number in my phone. I'm not sure I want to look yet.

I can't tell Mom about any of that, though. So I ask, "Didn't you ever wonder? Or ask Gram about it?"

She sticks the grocery receipt in the cookbook and closes it, and when she turns around her face is softer, memories shifting in her eyes, pushing her mouth into a wistful smile. "Sure. But I was also sixteen, and I didn't really care that much, you know? I wanted to *play*."

It stings a little—when my power started exploding out of me at all the worst times, huge and scary and thrilling, I didn't have Gram to guide me through it. Mom wouldn't talk about it and definitely didn't encourage me.

"I can see 'unfair, unfair' in neon over your head, you know," she says, and sits down next to me, her knee bumping mine, her pale hand reaching out to touch my cheek. "It wasn't right, keeping it from you, and I am sorry. You're my oldest, babe." Her smile is a little crooked, as regretful as it is fond. "I had no idea what I was doing as a parent, especially after your dad left. The magic on top of it, well . . ." She shrugs.

Her eyes are still focused on something I can't see, and I don't know whether she's remembering those horrible weeks when my power started to emerge, or when her own did, which was probably pretty cool, knowing Gram.

For a minute, I can almost see her as a kid, long-boned and pretty, dark hair swinging around her face, all the future years still ahead, nothing more than a vague idea of being grown-up. I smile and twist my hand around to squeeze hers.

She squeezes back, and I can tell she is sorry for how different it was for me. "You know the thing that scared me most?"

I shake my head, and she tilts her head as if she's trying to pick just the right words to explain it. "When my powers showed up, it was like being given the keys to a reliable, slightly dented, old Volvo. Nothing flashy, you know? But it ran, and that was enough."

"And me?"

She sighs. "Like someone handed you the keys to a really cherry, brand-new Lamborghini."

I roll my eyes at her use of "cherry," but I can sort of see what she means. What I don't understand is why I'm so different, and why Robin must be, too, since her power is already rattling in its cage.

But Mom is standing up, and the determined set of her shoulders means the conversation is over. *But only for now,* I tell myself.

She's getting out bowls and reopening the cookbook, and her tone is ruthlessly cheerful when she says, "I think Gram had some stuff collected somewhere about the family history. I bet Mari has it. I'll ask her to find it for you, okay?"

It's a compromise, but for now I'll take it.

I force myself to grin, pushing my questions to the back of my mind. "Okay. So. Let's make some cookies."

★ ★ ★

The house smells like warm sugar and vanilla, with tomato sauce on top, since we ended up ordering pizza for dinner. It also smells faintly like Mr. Purrfect, at least in the dining room, where I've stacked my books to study for exams.

What I'm really doing is cropping and resizing the photos I took this afternoon, using the laptop's crappy basic software.

"We need a new computer," I call into the living room, where Mom and Robin are watching TV.

"Gee, did I forget to shake the money tree again?" Mom calls back. "So sorry. Let me get right on that."

I sigh, and push the cat a few inches farther away. He's been sprawled on the table ever since I sat down, way too close to the laptop's keyboard for me, since he likes to walk across it if I look away. He sniffs, and I growl, "Go. Away."

I'm contemplating whether I can actually soup up the speed on the old machine when the doorbell rings, and my heart sinks.

Aunt Mari doesn't ring the bell, and it's almost nine, too late for any of Robin's friends to show up without calling first. I close the photo software quickly, and summon up my best innocent smile when Robin grunts, "Gabriel's here," from the front hall.

I wave him in, wishing I had at least one book actually open. Even a notebook. But it's too late, he's already walking through the living room, cheeks pink with cold, his pale hair windblown.

And he looks hurt. I don't think I'm imagining it, anyway, although it's hard to tell with him sometimes. If Mom can be a turtle when she wants to, Gabriel can be . . . I don't even know. Some weird creature that lives at the bottom of the sea in a cave.

"Hey." I stand up and take his hand, peeling off the glove to rub his frozen fingers.

"You didn't come by the store." His eyes are nearly pewter in this light, too dark, and unhappiness is thick in his voice. "Did you lose your phone?"

I pretend surprise, even though I suck at it. "Oh, wow. I must have left it up in my bag. And Mom and I were making cookies, and then we had dinner. . . ."

I sound open, I think. Open and honest and completely innocent, like there's nothing I'm keeping from him. Definitely not anything like the two kids who freaked me out for no reason earlier this afternoon.

I can see him wavering, his eyes searching mine as he pulls back the ESP that comes so easily. "I could be distracted with a cookie, you know," he says finally, and I grin.

"Wow, you're easy. I was thinking it would take a kiss, at least."

He grabs for me, but I'm too quick, twisting away from his reach and skirting the table to run into the kitchen, laughing.

"Oh my God, do you mind?" Robin yells, and I hear Mom's voice next, too stern and quiet to make out.

Gabriel follows me into the kitchen, and I swing the door shut behind him, stretching up on tiptoes to kiss him. I can't believe it was so easy to distract him, not when he's the one who's usually the worrier. And whatever happened last night seems distant now, with everything else on my mind. Anyway, that's not going to happen here in my kitchen, with my family in the next room.

I hope.

And it doesn't. It's just a normal kiss, which is awesome, especially when Gabriel fastens his hands on my hips to pull me a little closer. His mouth is still cold, but it's firm and a little demanding against mine, and he tastes like dark coffee. If I wasn't completely awake before, squinting at the computer screen, I am now.

"Hi there," I say when we break apart, and I actually have my breath back.

"Hi." He leans his forehead against mine before

kissing the tip of my nose, and then steps back to take his coat off. "Now give me my cookie."

I laugh and turn around to get one from the cooling racks on the counter, but I know Danny would have questioned me. Danny would have called the house phone, all "Dude, where are you?" Because there was nothing he didn't expect to know about me, or for me to tell him, even if he had no idea how many secrets I kept.

Gabriel never pushes, not really. Not when it comes to this thing between us. And I can't help wondering if it's because he doesn't want me to push back and ask him questions he doesn't want to answer.

I hand him one of each cookie, and he licks his lips. "No one'll notice if I take, like, a dozen home, right?"

"Try it and watch Robin attack," I say, and clear the empty pizza box off the kitchen table so we can sit down. "How was work?"

"Not as busy as Sheila wanted, I think." He pulls out the chair beside me, and leans in to kiss me again, a quick, sugary peck. "I guess the latest collection of horror stories doesn't really say 'Peace on earth, good will to men.'"

"Yeah." I lay my head on his shoulder, and swing one leg over his until we're all mixed up together.

"We should probably talk, you know," he says quietly, and for a moment I think he's poking into my head again before I realize he means about last night.

I sit up, but he keeps his hand on my knee, so I leave my leg where it is. "There's nothing to say. Whatever it is, I'll figure it out. And in the meantime, I don't think it's . . . dangerous."

Even I can hear how hopeful I sound. Because what do I know, really? We could go up in flames the next time we're making out, and based on last night, neither one of us would probably care.

"Don't you want to know what it means?" His voice is carefully even.

For a second I want to let loose, just shout at him. About how there are a lot of things I want to know, starting with all the things he never talks about. Do I want to know what it means when I kiss him and it feels like we're both turning into molten gold, melding together hot and smooth? Of course I do, since I'm not a complete idiot.

But what I want to know most is how he can stay so composed, so . . . grown-up, almost, when any other boy would let it rip, at least once in a while. And I want to know what made him so guarded, so reserved, that he clams up even when I can tell he doesn't want to.

"Look," I say instead, after taking a deep breath. "We have exams this week. I have to work tomorrow. It's not like we're going to have a whole lot of time to be . . . well, you know." I poke him in the ribs gently. "Okay? But I will figure it out, I promise. I figured out what I had to do with Danny, didn't I?"

The last part is whispered, since I never know when Robin will be lurking. And Gabriel smiles, the cloud in his eyes clearing long enough for me to see the boy I've fallen for so hard, the one who's smart and serious and funny in the most unexpected, dry ways. The boy who *is* just a kid, too, and worried about his girlfriend.

A boy who would most likely lose his shit if he knew a couple of strangers had caught me doing magic and then tracked me down.

But right now he's the boy who's leaning down to sneak one or two more quick kisses, hands clasped tight, before we're interrupted.

I hope wherever they keep track of this stuff, I'm getting extra points for understanding today. And that if Gabriel is still keeping parts of himself shut away, it's okay to keep a secret or two of my own.

# CHAPTER SEVEN

AUDREY DIEHL IS HANGING A POSTER ABOUT Adam's disappearance in the north hall Monday morning when I walk by on the way to my locker. His school photo is blown up in the middle of the page, and he smiles beneath the stark, bold MISSING above his head.

All Audrey's usual armor is gone. As far as I can tell she's not even wearing lip gloss. "Still nothing?" I ask her.

She shakes her head. "I sat with his little brothers most of the weekend while his parents were knocking on doors." Her smile is tight and sad. "It was even less fun than you might have guessed."

I had forgotten Adam had twin brothers. They're probably ten or eleven now, young enough to want promises that Adam will show up safe, and old enough to figure out that it probably won't happen, not after a week.

For a minute, the whistling hollow in my chest opens up, just like when I heard that Danny had died, and I have to swallow hard.

"I'm sorry." I don't know Audrey well enough to hug her or even touch her arm, but I want to help. "I can take posters, if you want. Put some up downtown and in Bliss. My boss would be totally cool with it."

Oh God, her eyes are filling up. I make myself stand there while she pulls a sheaf of flyers out of her bag and hands them to me. "Thanks, Wren."

She's already leaking tears by the time I grab the posters and head down the hall, and I have to hope Cleo or one of Audrey's regular entourage will show up.

I'm halfway to my locker when I see the dark back of a long wool coat down the hall, and I freeze for a second before I realize Bay doesn't go to this school. When the boy in the coat turns around, it's some senior laughing with a bunch of other guys.

Gabriel and I walk to homeroom together after we meet at my locker, and I stay close to him, glad of his solid warmth pressed against me. I spent most of yesterday at

Darcia's printing out the photos I took, and then at the café. Gabriel and I only managed to talk for a little while last night, and I missed him.

But I'm still not going to tell him about meeting Fiona and Bay. I definitely don't want to give him another reason to worry about me. And there's nothing to worry about, anyway. Bay and Fiona are just *kids*, like me, even if they do have power, but I haven't seen any evidence of that. They're probably wannabes with a Ouija board and a couple of grocery store herbs who think a few words in Latin are going to send them to another realm.

Gabriel faces me across the aisle when we sit down in homeroom, and I shove down all thoughts of everything that isn't his slow, gorgeous smile.

"French exam today?" he asks, crossing his legs at the ankles.

"*Oui.*" I nod. "That means yes, for the uninformed."

"Yeah, I got that, smart-ass." He grins wider and slides his foot across the linoleum to toe at my scuffed Doc. "How do you say good luck in French?"

I snort. "If I knew, maybe I'd pass the exam."

He rolls his eyes, and we both look up when Audrey walks in with Mr. Rokozny. She's clutching the flyers, and he waves her to the front of the room instead of into her seat.

"If everyone could take a couple of these and put

them up, that would be a huge help," she begins, and I have to look away from the raw grief on her face.

Audrey Diehl is the last person I would have expected to put so much into the effort to find a missing kid. Audrey's got the attitude, and the clothes, and a sweet little ride from her daddy, and usually a flock of boys fluttering around her like love-struck birds, but the truth is, she's not really as bad as all that. She's not purposely mean to anyone, and she's not completely shallow. It's more that into every high school a prom queen must be crowned, and Audrey was born for the role.

Still, despite the fact that I know she's more than her cheerleading uniform, it's surprising to see how seriously she's taking Adam's disappearance, and how personally. She grew up with him, true, but she's not sitting around weeping into her yogurt smoothie—she's actually breaking a sweat, spreading the word, babysitting for his brothers.

You never know what people are really made of, I guess, or what they'll do if you give them a chance.

When the bell rings and we all file out toward our first class, Gabriel takes my hand, his fingers warm and firm around mine. I hang on, watching as Audrey pushes down the hall in front of us by herself, flyers cradled in one arm, and her bag weighted down with more. She looks like she's heading out on a mission instead of to history or wherever she's going.

When I had the chance to do something right, with Danny, I did something horrifyingly selfish instead. I look up at Gabriel, who catches me and lets go of my hand to slide his arm around my shoulders. For a moment, my heart aches with both hope and regret.

I'm not going to let myself do anything like that again.

By Tuesday at lunchtime, everyone's twitchy with lack of sleep and general exam hell. I plop my tray down on the table in the cafeteria so roughly, my yogurt slides off one end, and Gabriel makes a big show of scooting his chair a few inches away.

"You're funny," I say in a tone that clearly indicates he's not, and sit down, dropping my bag on the floor.

For a moment we sit in silence, the tumbling wave of sound in the cafeteria rising and falling all around us, until I finally pick up my yogurt and peel the top back.

"Maybe he's not even gone," a sophomore in a loud plaid shirt says as he walks by with a kid I recognize from last year's art elective. "Maybe it's like, you know, what they say about hiding in plain sight. Like, he's around right here in town, but he just doesn't want to be found."

"Who would do that?" The other kid is skeptical, polishing an apple on the front of his jeans as they sit down at the next table.

I know they're talking about Adam, but I'm not

paying attention anymore. The yearbook staff is marching around the cafeteria, handing out pieces of paper.

"We need your help, people," Brittany Lowry announces as she leaves flyers on our table. Alicia Ferris is right beside her, although she glares at me. We've never liked each other, and the last time she actually talked to me I opened the sprinklers over her head.

Not that she knows that, of course, but still.

"We want the yearbook to be bigger and better than ever this year, and we need your contributions." Jess snatches up the hot-pink sheet of paper in front of her, squinting at it intently. "If you're a photographer or even have a camera—no cell phones, please—think about taking candids for us! We need them, and you can always start with your friends!"

They walk away to take their message to the next unsuspecting table, and I bite into my apple absently. I'm thinking about the look on Alicia's face when she ended up soaked, actually, until Jess says, "You should totally do this, you know."

She passes the flyer to Gabriel, and I roll my eyes. "Gabriel's not a photographer."

"I mean you, dummy," Jess says as if this should have been clear.

Now I'm glaring at her. Way to ruin my Christmas

photo surprise. She ignores me, of course.

"You take pictures?" Gabriel says, handing over the flyer with a curious expression.

I shrug. "I, uh, used to. Not really."

"See, right there," Jess says, leaning over the table to point at the words: MEETING MONDAY, JAN. 4, YEARBOOK ROOM, 4 P.M. BRING YOUR CAMERA AND EXAMPLES OF YOUR WORK. "You have plenty of time to get something together."

I blink at her. "Who said I wanted to take pictures for the yearbook?"

She's not backing down—I know that look. "No one. But I think you should do it, and Gabriel agrees. And so does Darcia."

"Darcia's not even here!"

"Yeah, but she would agree if she were," Jess points out, which is probably true. Even Gabriel is nodding.

I look at the paper again, thinking about how very much I do not have in common with Brittany Lowry and especially Alicia Ferris, but I think Tommy Britton is on yearbook this year, and I know there have to be other people. People who don't make me want to chew my own hair.

"I don't know. . . ."

"You can do anything," Gabriel says softly, leaning

a little closer so his words tickle my cheek, which is completely unfair.

"And it's not like you have to take pictures *with* them," Jess says carefully, as if she's talking to a slow four-year-old. "Because then you would all have the same pictures."

"Like they do every other year, you mean?" I ask her, and Gabriel snorts a laugh.

"It would look good on college applications," he says a moment later, while Jess makes dagger eyes at me.

"Yes!" She actually pumps her fist, and I kick Gabriel under the table.

He does have a point, though. I need more extracurriculars for my applications, and everyone from my guidance counselor to my mom to my boss at the café has started reminding me about it.

Plus, I could make Alicia's photos look really craptastic in comparison.

"It's a thought," I say with a shrug, and Jess throws a piece of green pepper at me. It still has ranch dressing on it, too.

"You're going to rock." Gabriel kisses my neck, right beneath my ear, and I shiver happily.

In World Lit, Darcia is sitting pale and nervous next to me as we start the exam, and I forget the extra, sharp pencils I had in my bag. I can't get them out once the test has begun, though, so I just keep writing, focusing on the tip every time it starts to round out, and watch as it sharpens itself.

No bells go off, no sirens blare, no one storms into the classroom in a black suit and FBI shades to take me away. Floating may have been a spectacularly dumb thing to do in public, but there are other things I can get away with.

I walk into PE and for the first time in my life, I realize I'm not dreading it. Just for the hell of it, halfway through the lesson on yoga stretches, I focus on a bag of gym balls propped loosely in one corner and concentrate on nudging it over just hard enough to fall. Balls bounce everywhere, half of them into girls pretending to breathe through the downward dog position. In seconds, the whole room is echoing with laughter, and Ms. Singer is barking to clean it up and go get changed, fifteen minutes early.

It ends up being a pretty good day after all.

Gabriel, Dar, Jess, and I push into the steamy warmth of Bliss after school on Thursday, the last day of classes. Trevor looks up from the counter with his usual scowling bad grace. "You're not working. To what do we owe the honor?"

I roll my eyes and drop my backpack on the window seat. "We're paying customers, isn't that enough?" I feel like I can really breathe for the first time in days, break is laid out in front of me like a clean sheet of paper, and not even Trevor is going to ruin my mood. The poster of Adam is sad, though.

He shrugs, and gives the others a tight smile before he turns back to the screen of his laptop.

"Was he born in a bad mood?" Jess says under her breath as she pulls out a chair.

"Yup. Get coffees and I'll go see what Geoff has in the oven. I want a mocha."

"Birdie." Geoff smiles when I walk into the kitchen, and leans over his worktable to kiss my cheek. He smells like flour and spices and fresh sweat, and the kitchen is even warmer than the café. All three ovens shimmer with heat.

"Anything good in there?" I crack one door to squint inside.

"Apple fritters and molasses crisps in a few," Geoff says, and stands back to brush his hands on his apron. The table is lined with four sheets of sugar cookies waiting to be baked, trees and stars and holly leaves smooth and perfect beneath crystallized sugar. "You here with Gabriel?"

"And Dar and Jess. Last day of school." I wet the tip of one finger and stick it in the colored sugar while he isn't looking.

He looks up and tilts his head, studying me a little too carefully. He's more than my boss, really, but sometimes the surrogate dad business makes me squirm.

"All set for Saturday?"

Of course, it would help if I didn't wind up telling him almost everything anyway.

"I think so." I wipe my stained fingertip on the back of my jeans. "I just hope Gabriel likes the pictures."

"Wren!" He rolls his eyes. "You've been together for months, sweetie. Anyway, any fool can see that he'd love it—"

"If I gave him a ball of hair. I know," I mutter.

"I don't know if I'd go that far," Geoff says drily, and waves me out of the kitchen. "I'll bring out cookies when they're done."

I have a little more than just the three framed photos planned anyway. I want to do something really special, something unique.

Something magical, in the literal sense.

For a couple of days there, I got so freaked out about being caught, I almost forgot how good it feels to use my power. And I don't want to stop—it's part of me, a big part of me, and that's not going to change.

Gabriel, and my mom, and probably anyone I asked would tell me I'm taking risks, using it at school, and here in the café last night, when Geoff was closing up the kitchen. But I was always in reach of the rag I had wiping down the counter on its own, and I was listening for him just to be sure.

It's not like I was going to make it rain over the cash register or turn a chair into a dog or something. Even though I'd pay serious money to see Trevor's face if I did.

When I walk through the door from the kitchen, Dar and Jess are laughing at the table in the front, heads bent together over something I can't see. Gabriel is sitting beside them, long legs stretched out in front of him, pale hair falling over his forehead, the beginning of a smile half hidden behind his raised cup of coffee.

Then he looks up and sees me, and his smile stretches out, warm and slow, the truth of it right there in his strange gray eyes.

Happiness is a sudden star flare, so perfect it takes my breath away. Even with Geoff banging around in the kitchen and Trevor grumbling at a customer, all I can think is, *Yes, this. I want to keep this.*

I push my hair out of my eyes, and let it come. It's nearly transparent, hovering in midair—a photograph, square and old-fashioned. The rippled edges make it look as if it's been torn from a sheet of paper. It flutters to the floor, and Gabriel, Jess, and Dar smile out at me from its face, soft and blurred like a wet watercolor.

It's a picture torn right out of my head.

I crouch to snatch it off the floor just as Geoff comes out of the kitchen behind me with a fresh tray of calories.

"Whoa, kid. Didn't see you down there." He skirts around me neatly as I cram the picture into my back pocket. I half expect it to crumble into nothing the moment I touch it, but it holds together.

I straighten up, the last hum of energy ebbing to a warm glow inside me. Gabriel's still smiling, not even a flicker of curiosity, so I'm pretty sure he didn't notice anything. I grab the mocha Trevor made for me off the counter before I join them. Geoff is handing around cookies and apple fritters, and Jess already has a glistening smear of frosting on her top lip.

"God, this is heaven," she groans, blushing when Geoff tweaks her ponytail.

*Heaven.* I sit down next to Gabriel, the photograph safe in my back pocket, and sigh when he pulls my hand into his lap, curling his fingers around it and holding tight.

It is heaven, here and now, and I don't see any reason I can't keep it that way.

# CHAPTER EIGHT

I'M PULLING A SWEATER ON WHEN ROBIN RAPS on my door Christmas afternoon. Mom and Mari are in the kitchen like a couple of demented elves, singing snatches of holiday songs and making so much food, we should probably invite the whole neighborhood over.

Robin opens the door before I can say anything, and I catch her reflection in the mirror. She's in new jeans, a dark purple sweater, and a scowl, but she's wearing the silver star earrings I gave her. It's something.

"They just pulled up." She leans in the doorjamb, arms crossed over her chest, not looking at me so hard her eyes are probably aching with the effort. I sigh.

She was better last night, when we all retreated to our rooms to wrap presents after take-out Chinese. Later, we piled onto the couch to watch *It's a Wonderful Life*. For the first time in years, Mari was with us, snuggled into one end of the sofa with an old quilt, weeping at "the richest man in town."

Gabriel totally owes me money, even if I didn't actually get a picture of her crying as proof.

"You look pretty," I say to Robin. Downstairs, I can hear the door open and the sound of Mom's voice, welcoming Olivia and Gabriel inside. And Robin does look pretty, all that thick dark hair washed and brushed, the new earrings sparkling when she moves.

Mostly, though, I'm hoping she knows enough to translate the compliment into what it really means, which is, *Make this any worse than it has to be today and you're dead.*

She shrugs and watches as I pull my boots on over new striped tights. "You do, too. I like your dress."

Then she's gone, running down the stairs before I can even look up from my laces. Or close my mouth, which has dropped open in shock.

There's no way to know if it's a peace offering or complete bullshit, but I don't have time to figure it out now. She's been running hot and cold for days, hugging me this morning when she opened her gift, bursting into tears late last night when Mom was talking about the plans for today. Some of it is probably hormones, and some is still pure tantrum that my boyfriend and his sister are coming for the day instead of our dad, and the combination is a nasty mix. I had to help her clean up the bathroom the other night when she melted the shower curtain in a rage.

I can hear everyone downstairs, so I stand up and glance in the mirror one last time. Aunt Mari gave me a beautiful charcoal-colored dress, and with my black and gray tights and tiny black sweater, I'm as dressed up as I ever get, even though I know Mom will roll her eyes at the sight of my Docs. I run my fingers through my hair, ruffling it one last time, and take a deep breath.

"There she is," Mari says when I walk into the living room. Gabriel is crouched by the fire, poking the logs, and Olivia is perched on the arm of the sofa, a big white mug in one hand. Robin's lying on the floor by the tree with one of the books she got this morning, and she doesn't bother to look up.

"Merry merry," Olivia says, and gets up to come give me a fierce one-armed hug. "Your aunt here is getting me drunk on eggnog already, just so you know."

"I assume they're hiding that pitcher from us." I blush when she kisses my cheek, but I don't really mind.

Mari pushes Olivia and me apart, all impatience and literally high spirits. "So tell me more about vinyasa," she says, pulling Olivia onto the sofa with her. I meet Gabriel halfway across the living room, and he kisses the top of my head.

"Hey there."

"Hey." I'm still blushing, and I don't even know why. Gabriel has been here dozens of times in the last few months, even if Olivia hasn't, and it's not like my family doesn't know him, or how gooey we can be together. But the day is as dressed up as I am, in its sparkling white lights and homemade cookies and pine perfume, and I feel like I'm waiting for a big glob of gravy to splash all over the front of it.

"Merry Christmas," he says, and takes my hand to lead me into the dining room. The table is mostly set in mismatched hand-me-down china, and tall, white tapers are nestled in the candlesticks, but it's empty otherwise. "What did Santa bring you?"

I roll my eyes, but he simply says, "Aw, just coal, right? It figures."

"Real cute." I get him this time, but he manages to grab my arm and pull me close. "I got a new iPod and a bracelet and two books and a gift certificate." I hold out my wrist, where the beaded bracelet Robin gave me gleams. She made it at a string-your-own place downtown, and it's all the shades she knows I love—filigreed silver and smoky hematite and black glass.

"Robin?" He glances into the other room, where Robin has abandoned her book to listen to the yoga talk, even though she's obviously pretending not to. While we watch, she frowns and tries to twist her lower half into a lotus.

The rush of fondness inside me feels good, like a steady candle on a cold day. "Yeah."

"I got her something." He sounds weirdly awkward, the way he almost never does, and when I glance at him, he's actually blushing. I'm still trying to process the surprise when he adds, "For your mom and Mari, too. And Olivia brought wine and stuff."

It's so unexpectedly sweet, I don't know what to say at first. So I say the stupidest thing, as usual. "Wow. One big happy, huh?"

Sometimes I am the blob of gravy on my own life.

He rolls his eyes, but he's not mad. There are some things even I can read without being psychic.

Mom comes out of the kitchen then, wiping her hands on a towel. "Food's almost ready, and I hope everyone brought appetites or you're coming back for leftovers tomorrow." Her smile is a soft rose flush in her face, and she looks about a dozen years younger somehow, not that she ever looks *old*. Even if it's just holiday happiness, I love seeing her like this. She swings the towel up over her shoulder and curls into the big chair near the fireplace, waving Gabriel and me into the room. "I'm so glad everyone's here."

"*Not* everyone," Robin says out of nowhere, her face tight as she untangles herself from her cross-legged place on the floor and stands up.

I expected gravy. But I didn't expect my little sister to practically launch a rotten turkey into the room.

"At least she didn't set anything on fire," I say to Mom after the brief storm passes. With the shouting and stomping out of the way, Robin is up in her room, simultaneously sulking and mortified.

"Yes, shattering half of the Christmas ornaments was so much better." Mom's voice is like sandpaper, and I push the vacuum back into the butler's pantry without another word.

In the living room, Mari is entertaining Gabriel and Olivia, or trying to, even though Olivia keeps saying it's not necessary. "Hey, I was that age once. We all were," she'd said.

Despite the months she's known me, though, I could

tell she was surprised by the sudden crack of exploding glass. At least she wasn't sitting close to the tree—Mom's hair is still sparkling with broken shards.

When I walk in again, Mari and Olivia are on the floor in front of the fire, talking so low I can't hear them, and Gabriel is rearranging decorations on the tree so the bald spots don't show. He looks up with a felt stocking in his hand.

"Hey. Do you think we should go?"

"No way." I take the stocking from him and hang it near the back of the tree—I made it when I was five, and it has nasty knots of dried glue all up one side. Not my finest artistic moment. "Mom is determined to have a nice meal even if it kills us all."

Gabriel mimes a weak fist-pump, and it's just enough to reset the moment to okay.

Mom sticks her head into the room. "How about some music and some food, people?"

"Sounds perfect," Olivia says, and gets up from the floor. Her face is flushed from the fire and probably the eggnog. "Can I help with anything?"

For once, Mom doesn't hesitate. "Absolutely. We need an army to carry everything."

We all pitch in, turning on music and bringing platters and bowls to the table, lighting the candles and running back to the kitchen for the salt and pepper. We're all seated before Mari says quietly, "Do you want me to get Robin?"

Mom unfolds her napkin and puts it in her lap, and it's hard to tell if it's only the soft glow of the candles making it look like she's blushing. "I told her to come down when she was ready to be polite, so if she's not here . . ."

There's nothing to say to that, so Aunt Mari pastes on a smile and says, "Merry Christmas, everybody. Let's enjoy."

There's ham and sautéed green beans and cheddar muffins and mashed potatoes and carrots with orange glaze, and for a few minutes everyone passes bowls and plates silently. Gabriel opens a warm muffin and pretends to faint.

"I love my sister, Mrs. Darby, but I have to say, she doesn't cook like this."

"It's Rose, Gabriel, and thank you." She laughs, and settles back in her chair. "Wren will tell you I don't cook like this most of the time, either."

"I'm learning," Olivia says with a stubborn twist to her mouth, but she's trying not to smile, I think.

"It has to be a lot to handle, working two jobs and being responsible for your brother." Mom's tone is casual, but I know where this is going. Another blob of gravy is going to drop any second. "Especially at your age."

Beside me, Gabriel's hand stops halfway to his mouth with a forkful of mashed potatoes, and I lay my hand on his thigh under the table as he says, "Olivia's really awesome like that."

"I'm just doing what needs to be done." Olivia lays down her fork and faces my mother across the table. "Same as anyone would."

"Well, not anyone," Mom argues, but at least her tone is kind. "A lot of people wouldn't."

"Our mom died when Gabriel was pretty young," Olivia explains. For all her wispy blond prettiness, her words are laced tight with steel thread. "And our dad is . . . not very reliable. And not very . . . caring. So yeah, I guess you could include him in the people who wouldn't, but I don't feel like I'm making a sacrifice. Gabriel and I do fine."

"No one's saying you're not," Mari says quickly, looking between Mom and Olivia. "Right, Rose?"

"Of course," Mom agrees, and shakes her head. "I probably sound like I'm interrogating you, and I don't mean to. But it's a little unusual for a twenty-three-year-old to have guardianship of her teenage brother. And I guess what I'm saying is, if you ever do need help, we're here."

Gabriel takes a deep breath, and I can feel the tension in him coiling tighter. "But you'd still like to know what the deal is, right?"

*Oh, no fair,* I think, and shudder at the idea of Mom realizing he's poking into her head. I haven't told her much about that at all, and I don't intend to—especially now.

Mom tilts her head, examining him carefully. "If I'm being completely honest, yes."

Time seems to stop, suspended like a flimsy piece of silk between moments. Gabriel hasn't even told *me* where his dad is, or what "unreliable" means when it comes to him, just that he and Olivia are better off without him. I can't believe this is suddenly the topic of conversation at Christmas dinner.

"We don't know where he is right now," Olivia says, and time crashes back into place. In her deep red dress with her hair piled on top of her head, she looks almost regal.

And not like someone who's going to cave easily.

"We haven't seen him in two years, and a few months after he didn't come back, I decided we weren't going to keep waiting," she goes on. Beside her, Mari opens her mouth as if she's about to say something, but I glare at her.

"I made some decisions about what would be best for

me and Gabriel, and as soon as I could I moved us here. The schools are good, and there's plenty of work." Olivia pauses, and then looks up at my mom again, and inside I'm cheering at the "don't mess with me and mine, lady" look in her eyes. "Wren's not in danger from him or from us. And that's really all I want to say on the subject."

It's so quiet, I can hear the fire sputtering and crackling in the other room, the soft shush of material as someone moves.

Gabriel looks stunned, when I glance sideways, but he's not looking at Olivia. He's looking at my mother. Who's smiling and is probably about to applaud, knowing her. She's all for girl power, no matter what.

But the silence is broken instead with, "Wow. What'd I miss?"

We all turn to find Robin slouched in the entryway to the dining room, nibbling at her thumbnail. She flicks her hair over her shoulder and adds, "Can I have dinner now?"

# CHAPTER NINE

"WELL, NO ONE DIED," GABRIEL SAYS FOUR hours later when we walk outside to sit on the porch. It's dark now, and the cold is knife-edged, slicing through our coats and scarves. "That's a win."

"Oh yeah. Taste the victory." I slide closer to him on the creaky swing and tuck myself under his arm. Inside, Mom and Mari and Olivia are sitting around the dining room table with coffee, and Robin is up in her room again, excused from further festivity after poking the fire and accidentally lighting up the curtains. The living room still smells like smoke.

"It could have been worse," he says, and kisses the top

of my head. His arm is firm and steady around me, and I bite back a sigh of pleasure when his fingers skate gently across my cheek.

Despite Robin's outbursts and Mom's awkward interrogation of Olivia, he's right. It could have been a lot worse, and in the end, the afternoon was actually sort of enjoyable. Comfortable in a way I hadn't imagined it would be, especially when Aunt Mari broke out the Pictionary and we all sat in front of the fire to play.

In fact, the only person who seemed a little off was Gabriel. He smiled and he made conversation and he played the game, but he was preoccupied, far away in his head whenever I looked at him, and I hated the fact that it was probably Mom's fault. Every once in a while I caught him looking at her, and the idea that he might not like her anymore tore at me.

But now he's wrapped around me, a blanket of boy in the frigid night, and it's good to let the moment stretch out. To gather it close just like his arm and soak up all of its warmth. To let myself think about what could come after tonight, where we could be next week, next year. All the things I had to stop dreaming about for Danny and me long before I wanted to.

My thoughts have carried me so far away, I'm startled when Gabriel speaks. "Did you want your dad here today instead?"

It takes me a minute to figure out what he's talking about. "No." I wriggle up straight so I can face him. "Not today. Today was about family, and my dad isn't part of that anymore. Not right now anyway."

As soon as the words are out, I realize it sounds like I mean Gabriel and Olivia *are* family, and I know I'm blushing.

It's a relief when all Gabriel says is, "I don't think Robin's going to wait forever."

I exhale, shaky and laughing. "Well, I'm not asking for forever. Just, like, another month."

He doesn't respond to that, and I'm glad. I don't want to think about my dad or Robin right now. So I sit up and reach for the package I set on the porch floor when we sat down. "I have something for you. Merry Christmas."

His grin is lopsided with surprise, and he leans over to kiss me. "I have something for you, too."

I sense Olivia's handiwork in the shiny green paper and the real white ribbon, but what's really nerve-racking is how much it looks like a jewelry box. I swallow and run one finger along the ribbon before I raise my eyes to Gabriel.

"You first," he says too quickly.

Okay then. I know Gabriel, right? It's not going to be a promise ring or something. At least, I hope it won't be.

I leave the ribbon curled in my lap and carefully

tear away the wrapping paper. He grabs it with a sigh of frustration, and I take a deep breath before I open the plain white box.

"Oh, Gabriel." The words are out before I can stop them, because the necklace nestled inside on its rectangle of cotton is beautiful. I pick it up with one hand, the long, silver chain cold on my bare fingers, and gently touch the objects dangling from it with the other.

A huge, old skeleton key, worn with age. A tarnished locket in the shape of a heart, at least as old as the key, with delicate scrollwork etched into the front. And finally a little silver bird, wings spread in flight.

I don't know what to say. Too many words are crowded in my throat, and I'm afraid if I let any of them go, the hot press of tears underneath them will spill over, too.

"This is you," Gabriel says, and I'm pretty sure he's ignoring my glassy eyes on purpose. He pushes the bird to make it swing on the chain. "I saw it in that antique store downtown, and then I just sort of went from there."

I stare at him, holding the chain so hard it digs into my fingers. "You made this?"

For a second he looks embarrassed. "Well, yeah. I mean, I saw the bird, and then I added the locket and the key. Is it . . . ? Crap, it's lame, right? I'm sorry, I thought—"

I grab his chin and kiss him, hard. "You thought so exactly right." I press the words into his mouth and lean my forehead against his for just a moment before I sit up.

Whatever he doesn't feel like he can share with me yet, this is Gabriel. This is the boy I'm falling in love with, a boy who gives me his heart and the key to it.

When I finally move back, he's smiling. "So you like it?"

I can't do anything but nod then, and hold the necklace up for him to take while I unbutton my coat. He lifts it over my head, and we both look down as it falls against my dress, charms clinking together softly in the quiet.

I'm *not* crying, I tell myself as I lean in to kiss him once more, and he thumbs one rebellious tear away without a word.

"Your turn," I say when I'm pretty sure I can speak again. "God, I hope you like this."

"Will you stop that?" He takes the box I hand him and laughs when I grab it back.

"Come with me. I mean, there's more, but not here."

He grins, sly and a little wicked. "I like the sound of that."

"Don't be a jerk—come on." I stand up and pull him down the porch to the front steps, and lead him into the backyard.

"I guess it's bigger than a breadbox, huh?" he jokes, and I roll my eyes. "Wren, did you get me a *car*?"

"You're going to ruin it," I warn him, but I'm smiling, too. The weepy romance part is over, and he doesn't look so distant anymore, either. For all I know, he was just worried that I wouldn't like the necklace.

There's an old wrought-iron bench set along one side of the garage, and I sit down there. "Okay, now."

He looks adorably confused, but he just shakes his head and tears off the wrapping paper to open the box. I take the lid from him and watch as his mouth opens in surprise.

"That's . . . my house. And my shoes. And *your* shoes."

"I took it." I can't help biting my bottom lip, hard, to keep my nerves from jangling so roughly inside. "I, um, took them all."

He's already lifting away the first frame to see the ones beneath, his mouth still open and his brow creased in concentration. "Wren, these are awesome. These are the kind of photographs you take?"

I poke him. "You don't have to sound so shocked. I used to take pictures all the time. Before . . . well, before. These are all places that remind me of us." *You too,* I hope but don't say out loud.

"I know. I don't even know what to say, they're . . .

they're really awesome." He looks up at me, and his eyes are so clear, so happy, it takes my breath away for a second.

This is it, everything I wanted, and nothing can ruin it, not Robin, not my mom, not my missing dad. It's a happiness so big I'm not sure I can even hold it.

I kiss him, because it's only going to get better now. I focus my power as I press my mouth to him for another second, and when I pull back I whisper, "Merry Christmas," and look out into the yard.

It's snowing, a slow swirl spinning lazily to the ground, and the bushes that line the fence are sparkling, tiny pearls of light hovering as if strung there. I reach out to let a snowflake fall into my bare hand, and it melts in an instant, fading into nothing but a faint wet smear on my palm.

*Just like a real snowflake,* I think, and glance up at Gabriel.

He's not smiling anymore.

"Too cheesy?" I say, trying to laugh. "Good thing I didn't go with the talking snowman."

"Wren, stop." His voice is a harsh scrape of sound in the silence, and his face is set like stone.

"I'm . . . sorry?" It's the most I can manage for a minute, and I turn away to focus again, winding the power back into its neat coil. The snow stops, barely a powdery dust on the dry grass, and the lights die with one last glimmer. "I . . . I thought you would like it."

He's already put the framed photos back in the box and closed the lid, and he sets it on the bench before he stands up. He only takes two steps before turning around, scrubbing at his face restlessly. Erasing something, I think absently.

"It's not that. It's . . . you have to be careful."

"What? Why?"

He stares at me and finally chokes out, "We're out in the open."

I can't believe what I'm hearing, not after the way we were together just a few minutes ago. "Gabriel, we're in my backyard."

"Right now, yeah." He stops pacing and fixes his gaze on me, so intent I couldn't look away if I tried. "But other places, too. I mean, I know you've been using it, Wren. I can feel it. Hell, I saw it, in the café the other day."

It's my turn for my mouth to fall open, but for a second I can't speak for the anger clogging my throat. I want to lash out at him with some snarky comeback, rip through him with words so sharp they'll hurt. But what comes out, in a small, hurt voice that I hate, is, "You make it sound like a drug."

He stops and looks at me, but even though I can see the regret on his face, I can't feel it. I can't feel anything but the cold and the numbing shock of his disapproval.

"I didn't mean it that way, really." He kneels in front of me, and I let him take my hand in both of his. I can't feel them, or him, either. I'm so cold, down to my bones, I feel like I might shatter if I try to move.

Gabriel's always known what I can do. He worried when he realized what I had done to Danny, but I don't blame him for that. I was wrong to bring Danny back, and I knew it.

But that's not what I'm doing with my power now. I made it snow. I made a moment in time into something I could keep, without a camera. This is not Black Arts or something freaky.

This is *me*. And he doesn't like it.

"Wren, please, you need to understand—"

I can hear his voice breaking, but it doesn't mean anything. His fingers twining around mine don't mean anything. I worked hard on the photos I took, because I wanted him to love them. But giving him this moment? That's what I was looking forward to. The magic I could share with him, and only him. That I *wanted* to share with him.

I stare into his eyes, dark gray now, the color of storm

clouds and slate, the color they turn when he's upset, concerned about me, trying hard to do the right thing.

But maybe it's just the evening's darkness. Maybe his eyes don't really change shades with his moods, and it's just a trick of the light.

Maybe it's all just a trick of the light.

"I understand," I say, and I'm proud that my voice is steady. "I understand everything. Good night, Gabriel."

I don't know when he and Olivia leave. I turn off my light and put my headphones on as soon I get to my room, and I stare at the wall beside my bed for hours, music unheard, more staticky noise in my head.

In the morning, sometime just after dawn, I take my phone out of the drawer in my bedside table and check the contact list.

I find J. BAYLISS there, and FIONA.

And I know exactly what I'm going to do today.

# CHAPTER TEN

MOM IS STILL IN HER PAJAMAS WHEN I'M getting ready to leave the house at noon. Curled on the sofa with a book, she looks up when I clatter into the front hall. "Going out?"

She sounds casual, but I know better. She was understanding enough not to bother me last night, and she still hasn't said a word about me blowing up the stairs without saying good night to anyone, but she's watching me. She's my mom, she gets to do that, and I understand that she's worried, but I don't want to talk about it yet.

"Yeah. I have my phone."

She puts her book down and stands up, grabbing her empty mug off the coffee table. "Meeting Jess and Dar?"

Damn it, I knew I wasn't going to get away without at least a couple of questions.

"Maybe later." I pick through the coatrack, looking for my other scarf, mostly so I don't have to face Mom. "I was going to meet some other people first. For pizza," I add, and could kick myself. Extra details are always a bad idea. I'm going to have to remember that I was supposed to be going to Cosimo's if she mentions it later.

"Should I ask if Gabriel is part of this plan?"

The fringed end of my green-striped scarf brushes my fingers when I push aside Robin's soccer jacket, and I grab it before I turn around. Mom has moved over to the front door, and she has her back to it now, as if she has all day to slouch there chatting. I sigh.

"It would be cool if you didn't. Ask, I mean."

She considers me for a minute, arms folded over her chest, her empty mug dangling from one hand. Her hair is piled on top of her head with a butterfly clip, messy and unbrushed, and in her robe and her old plaid pajama pants, she looks like a Sunday morning. Warm and comfortable and full of time. For a second, it's tempting to walk into her arms and let the whole ugly mess spill out.

But a part of me doesn't want to have to admit that

Gabriel is more narrow-minded than I expected. And a smaller part—minuscule, atom-sized—maybe doesn't want my mom to think less of him, because as mad as I am, I'm not ready to call him an asshole and start a smear campaign.

Anger is hot and bright, burning through everything it touches. You can warm your hands in the flames, at least for a little while.

A broken heart just hurts.

Mom sighs and comes over to hug me anyway, just long enough that I feel a little better but not ready to give in and burst into tears. "You know I'm here. And we can talk whenever you want, if you want to."

All I can do is nod. The sudden lump in my throat is evil and stupid, and I swallow it down hard.

She brushes hair off my forehead, and when she kisses my cheek, I breathe in the clean, familiar scent of her. "Have fun, okay? And let me know if you won't be home for dinner. We're all on leftover duty for the duration."

I sketch a salute. "Roger, corporal."

She snorts as she walks into the kitchen, calling over her shoulder, "Try four-star general, baby girl."

As if she has any better idea of military rank than I do. I wind my scarf around my neck and grab my bag, taking a deep breath before I walk outside.

If Gabriel isn't into the magical side of me, I'm going to talk to some people who might be.

I've never been to the coffee shop where Fiona wants to meet. It's on the other side of town, closer to the high school, and tucked in between a deli and a dry cleaner's. The sign looks like it was last painted in 1947 or so, and the inside of the place is just as retro, with cracked vinyl stools along a square counter in the middle of the room and a few ancient wood tables with matching chairs scattered along the walls.

Fiona and Bay are on the far side of the square, facing the front, and Fiona waggles her fingers at me when I walk in. A bell over the door jingles weakly, and I smile nervously.

The shop is deserted, aside from two old men who are actually playing checkers at a table in the front window, and neither one of them pays any attention to me as I walk by. There's only one person behind the counter, a girl in her late twenties who looks like she rolled out of bed only minutes after she climbed in. The front of her white apron is splashed with old coffee stains and something I hope is dried ketchup.

"A new face," she says idly as I take a stool next to Fiona. "It must be my birthday."

"Ignore Connie," Bay says with a sly smile. "She's permanently bitter. I'm pretty sure it's in her DNA."

She rolls her eyes at him and walks away, idly wiping the counter as she goes. And completely ignoring *me*, which I guess is okay for now.

Fiona jumps off her stool and ducks under the counter to scoop ice into a glass and pour some water over it. Connie doesn't even appear to notice, and Fiona grins like a naughty little kid. "We're very DIY around here."

She slides the glass toward me, and I stop it with my hand before it splashes my coat. Which I realize I should take off, as well as my scarf. I'm sitting so primly on my stool, all wrapped up, I must look like I'm at Sunday school.

I'm not like this, not usually, and if I'm going to hang out with these kids, I need them to know it. I figure acting the part will convince me, too.

"Nice," I say as Fiona gets back on her stool, spinning it lazily while I take off my coat and scarf. "You bartend in the Old West on weekends or something?"

It's weak, just a warm-up, but Bay laughs. "Fee here is just your average, everyday show-off," he explains, taking my coat as I realize I have no place to hang it. He gets up and carries it over to the row of hooks along the wall. "She likes to do everything with *flash*." He makes jazz hands in punctuation, and Fiona pouts.

"Everything's fun if you make it fun," she tells me, leaning close as if this is an important secret. Her breath smells like coffee and menthol cigarettes, and her lips are an iridescent plum today.

"I'm sure murder victims would love to hear that."

She looks so surprised for a minute, she doesn't respond, but Bay hoots out loud. "Oh, *snap*. This one's awesome, Fee."

It takes her a second to put her smile back in place, but once it's there, she doesn't seem mad. She pushes off with one foot and sends her stool spinning again, her cloud of hair bouncing over her frilly, white blouse.

She looks a little like something out of a Victorian picture book today, with her high-collared shirt and long, black skirt. But there's a black leather belt with silver studs around her waist, and black platform boots covered in zippers, so the effect is closer to a Victorian doll that a vicious little punk girl has dressed up.

"Do you want a coffee?" Bay says, and I drag my gaze away from Fiona with effort. She's got style, even if it's kind of deranged.

I lean over to look into his cup. "It looks like motor oil."

"Tastes like it, too, but it keeps you up." He grins and

points at the menu chalked in a careless scrawl. It hangs above the center island inside the square of counter, and it also looks like it was last revised before my mom was born. "They have food, too. As far as I know, it hasn't killed anyone."

"Cut it out, Bay," Connie says, and wanders back from the front of the shop with the old men's empty coffee cups. "You want a simple sandwich or a bagel or something, you're fine. I wouldn't suggest the meat loaf, though."

"Good to know," I tell her with a weak smile. "I'm not really hungry, though."

"But you are curious," Bay says, and I glance at Connie.

She's not paying any attention to us, rinsing the cups before setting them in the sink, and I nod at him.

"It's cool." Fiona slams to a stop by grabbing the counter. "We're not really here because of the munchies anyway, am I right?"

I glance at Connie again. I'm definitely not here for the food—I'm not sure I'll ever be *here* for food—but it doesn't seem like the stealthiest place to discuss the topic at hand, either.

"Hey, Con," Bay calls. "How about three of the giant mugs of tea, and a big piece of the cake?" He stands up before she's even turned around, and walks to the back corner of the shop, where a lone table for four sits with a sad, plastic daisy in a dollar-store bud vase. Fiona hops down to follow him, and I wind up scrambling behind them.

Fiona drapes her legs over the second chair on one side of the table, leaving me next to Bay. I manage to restrain a glare and sit down.

It was easy this morning. Fiona burbled and chirped at me and gave me the address of the coffee shop and that was pretty much it. Now . . . now is the part I'm less sure about.

"Fiona told me about what she saw in the tunnel," Bay says, and he doesn't even lower his voice. I have to clench every muscle not to glance over my shoulder at Connie. "But I guess you figured that."

"Yeah, pretty much. Who was your friend that day?" I ask Fiona. I can't quite dial my voice up to the normal volume, but I'm close.

"Oh, that was Neddie." She tosses it off and shrugs. "He's not around much."

"He's cool," Bay says, and leans back against the wall, one elbow up on the table. His coat is hanging on the wall next to mine and a yellowed rabbit-fur jacket I really hope is fake. I assume it's Fiona's.

I don't know what I expected Bay to wear under that

dumb coat. Black pleather? A three-piece tweed suit? But he's in a totally normal, gray button-down and faded jeans, and up close his face is friendlier and less mysterious than it had seemed after our one brief meeting.

I realize what he's said a moment too late, and I try to sound casual. "A threat? Is anyone a threat?"

He smiles, and even though it's simple, instantaneous, I can't help feeling that there's something lurking behind it. A shadow that flickers by too quickly to make out. "Not really, no. And Connie's totally taken care of."

Taken care of? I'm not sure I like the sound of that, but before I can steal a look at her, Fiona adds, "Simple spell. She doesn't hear anything we say about the craft." Her grin is pure delight.

I don't have to make up an excuse to glance at Connie now—I can hear her shoes on the faded linoleum floor, and when I look, she's carrying three giant mugs and a pot of steaming water.

"I'll be right back with the tea stuff and the cake. I assume you cheapskates—oh, I mean, poor, starving students—want three forks, right?" She looks exhausted, and her blue eyes are as faded as the floor.

"Absolutely!" Fiona chirps, and jumps up. "I'll help."

"So what kind of spell is that?" I ask Bay when they're gone.

"Nothing fancy." He shrugs. "Just takes the right wording. And some power." He runs his finger around the rim of one mug idly. "Do you use spells?"

"I have," I say carefully. No way am I saying what for.

His smile is just as slow as Gabriel's can be, but on him it seems practiced, like he's acting the part of the mysterious stranger. "But you don't always need to?"

I think of my mom, of Mari, of the kinds of things Mom has seen me do that startle her.

And then I think of Gabriel, and the way he balked at the show I put on for him last night without even a word.

"No."

Fiona comes back with the cake and the tea bags just in time to hear Bay say, "Oh, we're going to have some fun."

# CHAPTER ELEVEN

WHEN WE TUMBLE OUT OF THE COFFEE SPOT
an hour later, the chilly morning has turned into a
diamond-hard afternoon. The sky is bright blue, and the
wind is a sharp knife, Fiona is moaning and shivering in
her tiny jacket, and the whole thing seems hilarious and
perfect.

And I'm not thinking about Gabriel at all.

Bay looks sleek and sated, like a big cat, and he's still
licking the sticky ghost of cake frosting off one fingertip
as we head down the block. I don't know where we're
going, and I don't really care, as long as this sugar-high
happiness lasts.

"Do you know anything about glamours?" Bay asks, eyes scanning the sidewalk. There aren't many people around over here, not the day after Christmas.

"I've heard of them." I decide not to tell him where I've heard of them, as in movies and fairy tales.

He whispers something under his breath, looking over my shoulder at Fiona, and then back at me. "Hey, where'd Fee go?"

She's gone, and I whirl around, wondering if she ducked into a store. Knowing her, she's hiding behind a mailbox or something.

"I don't know," I say, and look back the way we came. The sidewalk is empty.

Then I hear Fiona's demented, delighted giggle.

"What did you do?" I ask Bay. In the scheme of things, making one girl invisible for a few minutes is nothing compared to raising someone from the dead, but he did it so quickly, so easily, as if he'd been doing it forever.

I want to know what else he can do. And what he can teach me.

He spreads his hand in the direction of the giggle, and the air shimmers for a split second before Fiona reappears, beaming. "So cool, right?" She claps. "Comes in very handy, let me tell you."

I can imagine, and for a moment an alarm bell goes

off somewhere in my head, but it's faint. I ignore it.

"Show me something," Bay says, nudging me with his shoulder. "Show us something."

"Here?" We're almost in the center of town again, and there are more people on the sidewalks, cars passing in the street.

"Sure." He shrugs, and Fiona turns around to dance backward in front of me, watching.

Both of them are acting like this is no big deal, but I'm nervous about being out in the open, not to mention performing on demand. I can't do anything too flashy, and I'm not sure I can do anything anyway—my mind is suddenly blank as I consider the green metal trash bin a few yards away, the traffic light, the sign above the candy shop.

Fiona pulls a cigarette out of her pocket and lights it, tilting her head at me sadly. "Come on, Wren."

I grab the cigarette out of her hand once she's taken a drag, and wave it in the air so it trails a thin, gray stream of smoke. Handing it back, I take a deep breath and blow at the hovering smoke as I concentrate.

It blooms like a flower, but instead it's a balloon, round and silver, with a shiny white string. It spirals up into the air with lazy grace, and Fiona hoots. "Perfect!"

Bay gives me the slow golf clap, with another practiced

smile. "Nice. I like someone who can think on her feet."

It sounds vaguely ominous, as if he expects us to be heading into battle or something, but I ignore him and walk ahead with Fiona, who loops her arm through mine. The echo of spent power tingles warm inside me, and I can't help grinning with pride. She looks over her shoulder at Bay before she says, "There's someone you should meet."

"Aw. Are we going to see the Wizard?" I tease her, and Bay laughs.

"In Fee's dreams, probably. No, just another friend. You'll like her."

For the moment, with the afternoon unfurling before me like big, gorgeous wings, I'm inclined to believe him.

We skirt the busy center of town and head into the neighborhood along its edge, where most of the actual apartment buildings are. There aren't many, and they're old and on the small side, but it's an old town. Bay cuts through the ragged front yard of a four-story brick apartment complex, and Fiona pulls me along behind him.

"Ring the bell, ring the bell," she chants, and Bay raises his eyebrows.

"Chill. We're not going to the circus, Fiona."

For the first time, she actually looks pissed off, but she doesn't argue. A minute later, someone buzzes us through the front door, and Bay heads upstairs.

Mari lived near here for a while, before she found the apartment she's in now, but this place in particular is a little seedier than I remember about this neighborhood. The halls are dark and haven't been painted in years.

Bay stops on the third floor and knocks on the door of the second apartment on the right. It takes a minute, which Fiona spends fidgeting and tapping her foot, but when it opens, a girl is standing on the threshold.

For a minute I wonder if they were messing around with me—this girl doesn't have the same air of mischief they do. She's sort of beige all over, lank, dirty-blond hair and faded corduroys and a light brown sweater, and she looks sort of like she's opening the door to the firing squad instead of friends.

"Jude." Bay leans in and kisses her cheek, pushing past her before she can invite us in. "Cheer up, kiddo. Where's your holiday spirit?"

"Wren, this is Jude," Fiona says, ignoring him, and I'm surprised she's the one to actually make introductions. "Jude, Wren is the girl I was telling you about."

"Oh, right." Jude summons up a weak smile and steps back. "Come on in."

Bay is already sprawled on the futon, flicking through what looks like a textbook. "Are we interrupting big plans?"

Jude stares at him for a minute, eyes flat, and the silence in the room is so heavy, I can feel all the air going out of the afternoon. "No," she says finally. "It's fine."

Fiona's already rummaging in Jude's small fridge. "God, don't you have anything not diet?"

"No," Jude says just as flatly as before, and sits down in a tattered easy chair that looks like it was a thrift-store special. "Hi, Wren. It's nice to meet you."

"Same here." I hope I sound convincing because nothing about this so far is remotely nice.

I'm trying to think of something else to say, but Jude does it for me. "Are you over at UCC? I don't recognize you from Summerhill."

Summerhill is the private arts college on the far edge of town, and I blink. "Um, no. I'm a junior. At the high school."

Jude looks surprised. "Ah." She glances at Bay, though, who simply smiles.

Fiona settles on the futon next to Bay with a big glass of orange juice. "I hated high school," she announces.

"Didn't we all." Bay sounds bored and puts down the book to sit forward and rest his elbows on his knees, as if he's waiting to be entertained.

*It shouldn't be a big deal,* I tell myself. That the rest of them are in college, or at least a few years older than me. It's not like I wandered into some official Grown-up Convention or whatever. But I can't help wondering if her reaction to me being in high school is as pointed as it seems.

Anyway, it gives me a chance to ask a few questions myself, which I haven't gotten around to yet. "Do you two know each other from Summerhill?" I ask Bay, and he nods.

"I'm a freshman, and I live in the dorm," he says, his eyes never leaving Jude's face. She's tracing the frayed arm of the chair with one finger. "Jude sort of adopted me last year."

"So you're . . . not a freshman?"

When she raises her face to me, the weary sadness there is impossible to ignore. "Nope. I'm a junior, too. Thought I'd try life outside the dorms for a while, especially since they're so small."

I'm not sure she got the better end of the deal—her apartment is tiny, and "dump" is a kind word for it, and since she's here today, all alone, she clearly didn't have money to go home for winter break. Maybe it's no surprise she seems so unhappy.

I smile at her, since there doesn't seem to be anything to say to that. "What about you, Fiona?"

"Fiona here is our resident dropout," Bay says. "Got herself kicked out of Saint Francis in her junior year, and is now a student of *life*." He intones the last part with melodrama, and Fiona rolls her eyes.

"I'll get my GED eventually. Maybe." She laughs and licks orange juice off her upper lip. "We've been showing off with the craft today, since we have a new playmate. It's your turn, Jude."

The way Fiona says "the craft" makes my stomach roll uneasily—it sounds too much like a weird, dangerous cult on her pointed pink tongue, and what's worse is that it sounds as if she likes it that way.

"You go ahead, Fee," Jude says with another weak smile. "You want something to drink, Wren? I have Diet Coke and, well, water."

I probably don't need the caffeine, but I want it anyway. Maybe I just want the buzz of discovery and freedom back. "I'll take a Diet Coke if you can spare it."

For the first time, warmth flickers in her eyes like a guttering flame. "Sure."

Fiona chants something that sounds like Latin, and a moment later, trembling strings of pink lights hang from the ceiling. She adds another word, and a butterfly like

I've never seen before swoops between them. It's huge, practically a small bird, and its wings are purple and blue streaked with white.

The fridge door shuts with more force than necessary, and I look up to see Jude coming toward me with a can of soda.

"Very pretty, Fee," Bay says, and stretches an arm along the back of the futon. "Isn't it, Jude?"

"Yeah, pink lights are just what the place needed." I hate how brittle her voice is—one wrong word and it's going to snap, slicing someone in half.

I haven't cracked open the soda yet, and suddenly I don't want to. I need to get outside, where the air is cold and clean and not so toxic. Whatever is going on between Jude and Bay, or Jude and Fiona, is none of my business. The shine on this day is going to wear off fast if I stick around.

I pull my phone out of my pocket, pretending it vibrated. I turned it off after talking to Fiona this morning, just to avoid the sound of Gabriel texting. "Oh wow. I didn't realize what time it was. I have a thing later. You know, family. I should go." I hand the soda back to Jude. "Keep it. I don't want to take a soda and run."

She looks relieved, but I have the odd feeling she's relieved for *me* and I can't understand why.

"We just got here," Fiona protests. She's already pouting, and her plum lipstick is smeared where she wiped her mouth.

Bay is regarding me silently, and I look straight back at him. I give him my best "want to make something of it?" face, and wave at the room in general. "I know my way home." I make it a joke, as if there's any doubt, and call over my shoulder, "Talk to you later. Nice to meet you, Jude."

The freezing chill of the afternoon is delicious when I step outside, and I breathe it in hungrily. The weird thing is, it was nice to meet Jude—she seems like an okay person. But I felt like I ended a daylong carnival by walking into a wake, and for someone I didn't even know.

New people are hard, I think as I head home. But not always bad—Fiona and Bay definitely aren't the villains I'd imagined them to be. Next time, I'll veto going to Jude's and let them work out their drama on their own time.

I'm daydreaming, wondering how to replicate those amazing lights, if not the slightly freaky butterfly, and before I know it I'm back in town, turning the corner onto Elm.

Where I nearly run smack into Jess and Darcia.

"Where have you been?" Jess demands. Her cheeks are pink with cold, and the shopping bag over her arm means she's been out spending gift certificates. "I've been calling you and texting you since last night."

"Did something happen?" Dar asks. She's bundled into a funny wool cap with a huge pom-pom and fuzzy red mittens. "How was Christmas with Gabriel?"

It's so good to see them—no matter how cool today was, Jess and Dar are practically extensions of me, but with them my thoughts of Gabriel come rushing back.

All I can think of is explaining what happened with Gabriel—or trying to, since I can't tell the whole story—and the day's last bubble of fun pops. I can pretend I didn't use Fiona and Bay to ignore what happened with Gabriel, and it might be partly true, but not completely.

I don't know what shows on my face, but before I can form a coherent response, Jess grabs my chin and looks at me closely. "Uh-oh. You look like you could use a mocha. Come with us."

I might not want to spill all the ugly, upsetting details of my fight with Gabriel, but I know one thing as I let Jess march me toward Bliss—being with the two of them is much better than being alone with my thoughts of him.

# CHAPTER TWELVE

I KNOW I CAN'T AVOID GABRIEL FOREVER. BUT for the next two days, I manage to do a pretty decent job.

With Jess's and Dar's help, of course. Jess treats us both to a movie the night I run into them in town, and on Tuesday, Dar comes over to help me clean my room. That one was Mom's idea, and I'm pretty sure it's supposed to be a distraction, but I don't really mind. It's a pit anyway, and I find three shirts I thought the washing machine had eaten, and a history paper I never turned in.

I don't tell Mom about that.

It's not bad—we turn music on, and Robin comes in for a while to sit on the bed and make snarky remarks about slobs and other lower forms of life, but I don't shoo her out. She loves Darcia, and I figure if I'm not ready to call our dad yet, I can at least throw her a smaller bone.

"You are so lucky," Darcia says, sitting on the bed next to Robin and stroking her thick, straight hair.

"Are you kidding?" Robin says, but she's blushing. "I love your hair. It's a lot like Aunt Mari's."

"I see no one wants *my* hair," I point out. "Thanks. Also, no one is helping anymore."

"We're taking a break," the two of them say in unison and laugh.

I groan and turn back to the bookcase I emptied out all over the floor, and my phone buzzes in my pocket.

I can't keep it off all the time, since Jess and Dar are apparently on Wren Watch and need to be in touch every minute, but I'm always afraid it's going to be Gabriel. He stopped leaving voice mails by Monday, and the texts are coming in a little slower now, but he hasn't given up entirely.

I can't decide if I'm secretly happy about that or not.

But it isn't Gabriel—it's Bay. Crap.

I wander into the hallway casually, since Robin and Dar are still cooing at each other's heads, and answer. "Hey."

"What's with the disappearing act? I thought we were making friends." He sounds far away, his voice crackling.

"You texted me this morning and I answered you," I say. "Don't pull a stalker on me."

He laughs, and I can hear Fiona in the background, shouting something about balloons. "No stalking. Just wanted to hang again. You up for it?"

I bite my bottom lip and glance back into my bedroom. Mom already announced she was getting stuff for homemade pizza tonight, and Jess is coming over later. Mari, too, with a new DVD. There's no way I can get out of it.

"Maybe Thursday afternoon?" By then I can probably make up an extra shift at the café, even though Geoff gave me most of the week off with pay for my Christmas gift. "I'm not ducking you, I swear."

"Hmmm." He hushes Fiona then, and says, "I suppose the fairy princess over here can wait. But if she shows up on your doorstep, don't blame me."

Well, that idea is completely terrifying, but I decide to believe he's joking. "I'll call you."

"You better. I want to see what other tricks you can do."

I laugh. "Better than balloons, I promise."

"Who was that?" Dar asks when I go back into my room, and I shrug casually. Dar never thinks anyone has a secret—or a reason for keeping it.

"Ryan. Just checking in about Becker."

Her mouth forms a perfect O of pity, the way I knew it would. Becker still hasn't come back to school, and the last time I saw him, he was so high on pain pills he could barely keep his eyes open. No one knows what to say when it comes to him, so most people just don't say anything.

The lie feels dirty, even if it's just a little one. After everything that happened when Danny died, I promised myself no more secrets, no more keeping anything I didn't absolutely have to from my friends.

But now . . . I stuff my phone into my pocket, and my guilt with it.

I turn the corner onto Dudley at eight o'clock on Thursday night, where Jess and Dar are supposed to be waiting for me. Noah Strickler's parents are skiing in Vermont, and he's having the kind of enormous open house that everyone goes to, no matter who you are. Noah's house is epic, and so are his parties. His parents are, I guess, either clueless or completely unconcerned, even though the house usually smells like it was marinated in beer the day after one of his keggers.

Jess and Darcia are waiting, as planned, huddled together in the cold, but they're not alone. Gabriel is standing with them, a tall slash of boy in the darkness, moonlight on his hair.

And the carefully built wall that had been keeping all my feelings about him safely hidden starts to crumble, right there. I can feel the first crack whispering up from the ground and the bricks shifting and breaking.

It's all I can do not to scream or cry. It's even more of an effort not to turn and run.

"Wren, just . . . just give him a chance, okay?"

From Darcia, I might have expected it. Dar believes in happy endings and refuses to admit that anyone doesn't deserve one. But Jess? I thought she was going to be on my side.

"There are no sides," Gabriel says quietly, and my hands curl into fists.

"No fair." Jess and Dar will think I'm talking about their meddling, and that's okay. I'm as mad about that as I am that Gabriel is already poking into my head.

"We just wanted to help," Darcia says, walking up and bumping me with her shoulder. I can't decide if I want to hug her or squash her. "We thought maybe if you had a chance to talk . . ."

"Sometimes it's not that easy," I tell her, but I'm looking right at Gabriel.

He looks awful. Pale and sort of pinched, as wrecked

as I could ever imagine. Like maybe he has a wall that's cracking, too, and it hurts.

"There's a party to get to, people," Jess points out. She's stamping her feet to stay warm. "You guys can talk on the way. Consider it a Christmas gift. To me."

Even Gabriel rolls his eyes at that, and I can't help it, I want to climb all over him and laugh with him and kiss him. It turns out it's hard to hold on to a mad for five days.

The hurt is going to last a while, though.

"All right, walk," I say, and Dar and Jess set off together, carefully ahead of Gabriel and me. The pom-pom on Dar's hat bounces as they go, and Jess lights a cigarette.

Beside me, Gabriel is tall and quiet and so close. I hate the completely inappropriate urge to slide in even closer and let him wrap me up with one arm, the way I would have done a week ago. "Wren, I want to explain," he starts, and I hold up a hand to stop him.

"Me first."

Out of the corner of my eye, I see him nod, and he looks so miserable, nearly haunted, that a little more of the ice around my heart melts. But I don't want to give in completely; I *won't*.

"You really hurt me," I say, proud that my voice is steady. "That was *me* that day, Gabriel. I mean, I took the pictures, yeah, and I wanted them to be special, and I really wanted you to like them, but I could have given the same kind of gift to Dar, or Jess."

He frowns, and I plunge ahead. "But when I made it snow, that's not something I can do for anyone else except my family. Not even my friends, Gabriel. I can share stuff like that with you not just because you know about it but because I *want* to. Do you get that at all?"

"I do." The words are choked with regret, heavy in the silence.

I shake my head, trying to understand. "Then why . . . ?"

He puts a hand on my arm, and I stop, letting the others turn the corner ahead of us. When I look up, I think I can see everything Gabriel is in his eyes—warm and true and sweet, but troubled, too. There are shadows there, and in them the shapes of fear and loss and helplessness.

"Because I love you, Wren," he says, and I can hear my breath escape, the softest gasp of surprise. It shimmers in the cold air. He's never said that before—*we've* never said it before.

I don't even have time to process it, though, because he's still talking, one hand still resting on my arm, not tight, not possessive, just there, connecting us.

"There's just a lot you don't understand yet about your power, Wren, and when you use it . . ."

I tip my head back, focusing on the cold sky, the glittering pinpricks of stars. "And you do?" I say when I finally look at him again. "Gabriel, you don't know any more about it than I do. It's just power. *Magic.* It's natural, for me at least, and my family. I'm not some ticking bomb, you know. I'm only a girl."

"A girl who can raise her dead boyfriend from the grave," he reminds me, and that's when I shrug his hand away.

"I learned my lesson. And I can control my power now, you know that." I take a step back, crossing my arms over my chest. "Stop worrying about me, Gabriel. I have a mom for that. I have *me* for that. I want you to like me, *all* of me." Then, before I can think twice, "I want you to love me."

He rakes his hands through his hair. "And when you love someone you worry about them. I don't see what's wrong with that!"

Suddenly the cold night is reaching inside my coat, into my bones and blood, and I don't think it's just the temperature. "I made it snow for you, Gabriel. I made it . . . beautiful. And what's wrong is that when it comes to my power, all you do is worry."

I leave him standing there and run to catch up with my friends.

# CHAPTER THIRTEEN

NOAH'S IS PACKED, PEOPLE AND LIGHT AND noise spilling out onto the frozen lawn in front, and huddled in half-drunk, shivering circles around the covered pool in back, smoking. I give it another half hour before a drunk sophomore tries to walk across the tarp.

Music is blaring in the living room, and someone has moved all the dining room furniture to one side so people can dance. Jess heads off in search of Noah, as if saying hi to the host is really an issue, and Dar sticks close to me as we push through to the kitchen.

Gabriel trails along behind us at a respectable distance of about six feet.

I hate how much I love that he's not giving up.

"It's really crowded," Dar says, and I can barely hear her above a bunch of senior guys laughing and hooting over the keg. I grab her right before a spray of beer arcs across the kitchen, and she groans.

When I look over my shoulder, Gabriel has been cornered by Brian Sung and Phoebe Gleason, who can spot a guy fighting with his girlfriend at five miles. She already has one hand on his arm and her cleavage exposed, and I want to pull her out of the house by her shiny, over-conditioned hair and pounce on her. Hard.

Not that I'm jealous, of course. I'm not even worried, since I know in my bones that Gabriel wouldn't cheat. But I still don't like the way she's hanging all over him, in her perfect little outfit with her perfect not-so-little breasts, or the way she's telegraphing "available for random make outs" in huge, neon letters.

Gabriel's attention is focused strictly on Brian, though, and in another minute Phoebe loses interest and wanders away.

"See?" Darcia whispers, still clinging to my jacket with one hand. "Nothing to worry about there."

"I wasn't worried," I snap. *Not about that,* is what I don't add. Instead, I pull her toward the family room. The sweaty press of bodies all around is already too hot.

The French doors off the family room lead out to the patio, where there are coolers full of soda and more beer, and the cold is biting and welcome after the crush inside. Dar wipes down a diet cola with the sleeve of her jacket and cracks it open, sitting on the low stone wall that borders the patio.

"Why are we here again?" she asks me, trying to smile. This kind of thing is never her idea of fun.

"To have a good time," I inform her, and grab a bottle of beer out of the other cooler. I'll just have one, because I know what can happen if I don't stop, but I don't mind the idea of a little buzz for now.

"You don't have to babysit, you know," Dar tells me when I sit down beside her. "Go have fun. Or even better, go find Gabriel and talk some more. Isn't that a good idea?" She makes a hopeful puppy face, and I snort.

"I'm not babysitting, I'm hanging with my best friend." I bump her shoulder companionably with my own, but I'm restless. I spent the afternoon running around the deserted park with Bay and Fiona, showing Bay how I could levitate, turn brittle, brown leaves into pinwheels, and make a shimmering carpet of pine needles.

There's nothing like the feeling of magic running hot in your blood. It's like being made of light, silver shimmering in every cell. In comparison, the party feels like nothing but noise and confusion.

Meg D'Angelo wanders toward us, nodding at Dar before she sits down. "I've got a pool going on who pukes first. Want in?"

That startles a laugh out of me. "No, thanks. I'm tapped out at the moment."

She nods. "Yeah, well, me too. Why do you think I'm running it?"

Darcia stands up abruptly. Her chin is set firmly, and I watch her squaring her shoulders like she's preparing for battle. "I'm going to go . . . mingle. Just so I can tell Jess I did."

"Good girl." I raise my beer, and Meg does the same. As I watch her push back into the crowd, I tell myself I'm not looking for Gabriel at the same time, and either way, I don't see him.

Meg saves me from that by asking if I've heard the new Pilots song. We spend the next half hour slowly drinking our beer and discussing the incredibly lame music being played by whoever's in charge of the sound system. At one point, a couple of sophomores walk by talking about Adam, and Meg and I fall quiet for a few minutes. We're both shivering, teeth chattering around the wet mouths of our bottles, when Jess plops down beside me.

"Hey, you," she says, and grabs my bottle to down the last little bit.

Meg nods at her, and Jess nods back, and I frown at Jess. "That was my beer, you know."

"I tell myself a sip here and there doesn't count as long as I don't grab a bottle for myself. Anyway, the keg's already spent." She's pink-cheeked and pretty, eyes bright with happiness and a faint smear of alcohol, and I grin at her.

"Where's Dar?" She twists around to scan the crowd around the pool, her ponytail just missing my cheek.

"She headed inside a while ago. Which I should do, because I'm freezing and I need to pee," I say, standing up. "I'll find her."

"What did you think of the Brown brochures?" Meg is asking when I walk away. She and Jess aren't exactly friends, but Meg is another not-so-secret brainiac who's going to end up somewhere with ancient ivy crawling up the walls.

I spot Gabriel and Brian sitting on the stairs, each with a half-full beer. They're talking so intently that Gabriel doesn't notice me, which I decide is a good thing. I cut through the packed living room and peek into the dining room, where a couple of junior girls are dancing to Kesha, but no Darcia there, either. The last thing I want to do is go up the stairs, which would mean practically climbing over Gabriel, so I decide to look out front before circling around to the back and into the kitchen.

A few freshmen are sitting in the driveway, passing around a lone red cup, and Jenny Carpenter and Greg Nowak are tangled up in a redwood deck chair someone dragged into the middle of the front lawn. Her shirt is half open, but since his hand is inside it, I figure she's probably plenty warm enough.

I don't look over toward the garage until I hear voices, and then every hair on the back of my neck bristles. Cal Gilford is there, looming over Dar in an actual letterman jacket, like every bad cliché from an after-school special ever written. She has her back up against the garage door and her face tilted up to him, and even from a distance I can see the reflected gleam of tears in her eyes.

Oh, *no* way.

I don't think twice, just unleash my power in a gust of wind that sends a formerly nonexistent basketball rolling off the roof onto Cal's head. It lands with a nasty thunk, and he staggers backward, yelping. His red cup of beer splashes all over his jacket, and he winds up on his ass in the driveway, shaking his head and swearing.

And Darcia is . . . leaning over to help him, horrified, checking for a lump.

She's supposed to be running away, because Cal, who's supposed to be crushing on Jess, was making a move. I think. I *thought*. Crap.

I swallow hard, and walk toward them, pasting on my best innocent face. "Everybody okay?"

"Sort of?" Dar says, and tries to wipe beer off Cal's jacket with one of her mittens. "A basketball rolled off the roof!"

"Those things are harder than I thought," Cal grunts, and stands up. "Hey, Wren."

Before I can say anything else, Darcia cuts in. "That awful Jimmy Coes was being a . . ."

"A dick," Cal says distinctly, and rubs his head again with a wince. "Had her practically pinned up against the door. Fucking drunk little geek. He took off down the block, probably puking all the way."

"I'm going to have beer-breath nightmares for days," Darcia says with a shudder. "Why can't anyone normal have a secret crush on me?"

I'm pretty close to puking myself. *Way to get every last detail wrong,* I tell myself, and realize someone is standing just behind me. I turn my head and there's Gabriel, looking very sober and completely grim.

Perfect.

"You okay, Dar?" Gabriel says, and she nods. The

color is coming back into her cheeks, even if she's holding one beery mitten by its thumb like it's toxic.

"Cal scared him, for life, I think. I almost feel bad."

"Well, don't," Cal says. "I'm going to, uh, get some ice, I think. Or maybe another beer. No pain, right?" He laughs as he ambles toward the house, the beginning of a spectacular blue egg on his forehead.

"I'm going to make sure he's okay," Dar says with a worried smile. "And tell Jess he should get extra points if she's still keeping track."

Which leaves Gabriel and me standing in the driveway alone, with the basketball in a puddle of spilled beer. This is definitely not my idea of a good party anymore.

"What did you do?"

"I don't actually report to you, you know," I say, and cross my arms over my chest. I'm already mad at myself. I don't need him to join in.

He scratches his head, still frowning. He's wearing my favorite of his shirts, a dark blue button-down that makes his eyes look startlingly gray. Through the steam of anger, I wonder if he wore it on purpose. "I'm just saying, this is the kind of thing that could get you in trouble. I mean, what if you really hurt him or—"

"But I didn't." I step closer, straightening my spine. "I feel awful about it, okay? But I thought he was hurting her. Plus, he's supposed to be all in love with her best friend! And anyway, she *was* being hurt, just not by him."

It's a stupid explanation, and I know it, but now I'm mad at both of us. Clarity has never been a strong point when I'm vibrating with anger.

"You could have walked up to them, you know, or yelled," he argues, keeping his voice low. In the reflected light from an upstairs window, his eyes are dark as slate, and in each one is an accusation.

Tears are hot in my eyes now, and the lump in my throat is going to be hard to talk around. "Well, I didn't, okay? And I don't need you supervising me every minute. I know I screwed up, believe me, but thanks *so* much for making sure to drive that point home a couple more times."

He clenches his jaw. "Wren, you don't—"

I let it come, fury and hurt whipping together inside me until I have to let it out. "You're right, I don't." A sudden wind swirls up around us, tossing leaves and stray twigs at our feet, a personal storm. "Whatever you're going to say, I don't. I don't *care* what you're going to say, and I *don't* want to talk to you anymore."

"Wren, please." The agony in his voice would be hard to walk away from if I wasn't so furious.

"Just stop," I tell him, and let my anger shatter

the lightbulb in the fixture over the garage door in punctuation.

He looks wrecked, lost, and I can't tell whether he's having another headache or if he hurts somewhere a little deeper.

"Wren, you have to see this," someone calls from the front yard, and I drag my gaze away to see Meg arm in arm with Jason Carlson, cracking up. Jason graduated last year, but a lot of kids are home on break and not too proud to come to a high school party. I didn't know he and Meg were still together.

Gabriel runs a hand over his face, and I want to walk away, but I also want to throw my arms around him. I'm so tired of being torn.

I'm still wavering when Gabriel hisses, "Just go."

I swallow back a protest and walk over to Meg and Jason, who bends to kiss my cheek. He's got a new tattoo and an even newer black leather jacket on, and Meg tugs at my hand.

"Seriously, come on, two of the juniors on the wrestling team are stripped down to their tightie-whities and going at it in the backyard."

I let myself be dragged along, even though I can't think of anything I'd rather see less. Halfway around the side of the house, I see Brian whispering something to a girl I don't recognize, and I snatch my hand out of Meg's.

"Hey," I say to Brian, pushing into their space. The girl blushes and licks traces of smeared lipstick off her bottom lip. "Gabriel is . . . I don't know. He's out front by the garage. Could you . . . ?"

"Um . . ." I make Dar's puppy eyes at him when he hesitates, and he shrugs and nods. "Sure. I'll give him a ride home. Wanna come?" he asks the girl still snuggled into his side, and as I walk away, she's beaming.

There, done. At least I know he'll have a way home.

But I wait out the rest of the night on the wall in the backyard with a red cup of water, by myself. For me anyway, the party's over.

# CHAPTER FOURTEEN

DARCIA HAS CUPS OF CONFETTI AND NOISE-makers and glittery party hats laid out on her dresser.

"I don't care if you think it's lame," she warns Jess, poking her shoulder. She's already in pajamas, faded blue-plaid flannel pants and an old gray sweatshirt. "It's New Year's Eve, and I want to celebrate."

"You're a party animal, *chica*," Jess says, and dumps her duffel bag in the corner of Dar's bedroom before kicking off her shoes. "I assume the hookers and blow will come later, right?"

"Jess!" Dar exclaims, blushing.

I bite back a laugh, but I say, "Don't be a bitch," and

throw my backpack at Jess even though we all know she's just kidding.

She catches it and tosses it back, grinning. "Just trying to get the party started."

And I'm trying my best to get into the mood. We're sleeping over, which we've been doing forever on New Year's Eve, and I don't want to ruin the night by brooding. But I haven't spoken to Gabriel since the party at Noah's the other night, and I can't erase the image of his face, twisted in pain.

Not that it matters. I'm not going to be someone I'm not just to please him, and I don't want a boyfriend who thinks he knows better than I do what's right for me. My heart just hasn't quite gotten the "stop loving him, you idiot" message yet.

I don't think hearts really work like that anyway.

I've been trying to distract myself. I took about a zillion pictures of the dumb cat to make Robin happy.

"Oh, he's a natural," I said at one point when he yawned at me, whiskers twitching. "Look at him working it." We were in her bedroom, and she'd posed him on the deep windowsill, so he would look soulful and wise, according to her.

I thought he still looked like a vaguely overweight lump of orange fur, but I didn't say that.

"Take one of us together," Robin said after I'd snapped a few more shots. She scooped him up and sat down in her desk chair, holding him up to her chest and burying her nose in the fur at his neck. Her big brown eyes were shining, and I had to smile.

"'A Girl and Her Cat,' I'll call it," I said, crouching to get a better angle. "Maybe I'll print it in black and white, make it totally arty."

As if, of course. It was going to look like a thousand other drippy cat pictures on the internet, but Robin didn't have to know that.

"Let me see," she demanded when I'd taken a couple. She let the cat go, and he stalked off the bed in a hurry. I handed her the camera, and she clicked through the pictures on the screen.

"Oh, this one," she announced. She was biting her bottom lip, like a grin too big would crack her face open.

She turned the camera around to show me. It was a cute shot and even though I didn't think it was exactly groundbreaking, it was enough to make her happy.

I was about to suggest trying something else, maybe doing her up gothy or like an old-time movie star, just for fun, when she said, "When you print that one, I'm going to send it to Dad."

The bottom dropped out of the moment then, all the

air in the room whooshing past until I was dizzy.

"What . . . why?" I managed.

"Because I want to." She crossed her arms over her chest, chin stuck out like a dare. "Because he's my dad, too."

"Robin." I took a deep breath, trying to find the right words. "Do you get at all that I'm worried about you, too?" It felt so wrong to say it, after telling Gabriel he had no right to worry so much about me, but it was true. "You were a baby when he left, Binny. And I don't know who he is in your mind, but if he doesn't live up to that . . . if he left because he was selfish or didn't care, I just don't want your heart broken."

"I'm a big girl, Wren." Tears were already shining in her eyes, but she was standing up straight, defying me to tell her differently. Stupid kid. She was more like me than she knew.

So I left her there, with her cat and her dreams, and shut myself in my room for the rest of the afternoon.

That night, all I wanted was a way to keep busy. I called Fiona, and we went into town with Bay to see a movie. We were early for the nine o'clock showing, so we walked around aimlessly with coffees. There were posters about Adam in almost every window, and I couldn't help thinking about his family, missing him and aching.

Only the restaurants and cafés were open, so the

AMY GARVEY

sidewalks weren't exactly crowded, but every time Bay made a window-display Santa dance or repainted the lettering on a sign with silver glitter, my heart pounded. Fiona was chattering about what the block between Elm and Quimby would look like if it were all pink, and even Bay rolled his eyes at that, although he did let her turn one metal garbage bin into a cupcake. It was reckless, way more than an afternoon in the deserted park across town, and nothing I did drowned out the sound of Gabriel's voice in my head, warning me to be careful.

But tonight it will be easier to forget Gabriel entirely. Dar's mom always provides enough snack food to feed a battalion, and there are a dozen different movies we can watch, piled together on Dar's bed with the lights out and a zillion pillows to snuggle into. I'm secretly hoping for one of our infamous Scrabble battles, too. Dar isn't as vicious as Jess and I can be, but she loves to egg us on, and sometimes even makes words she knows we'll be able to build on.

Jess and I play practically to the death. One time when I won by only three points, she tackled me to the floor and tickled me so hard I could barely breathe.

I drop my bag beside the bed and sit down to untie my boots. Pajamas are the first order of business, and I rustle through my bag to find the black leggings and big shirt I usually sleep in.

161

Jess is already changing into hers—purple thermal long johns—and from inside the shirt she's pulling over her head, I hear, "I saw Cal last night."

Dar settles on the bed cross-legged and claps her hands. "Tell all, please."

"Not much to tell." Jess emerges from her shirt, pulling it down into place and then reaching up to straighten her ponytail. A sly smile twists her mouth into a lopsided comma. "Except for the fact that he's a really good kisser. Like, epic. The boy should win an award."

Darcia squeals, hugging her knees to her chest. "Okay, now you really have to tell all. Especially since my last kiss involved a freshman in the chess club who tasted as much like old tuna fish as he did like beer." She shudders.

Jess screws up her face in some weird combination of pity and disgust. "Anyway. So yeah, we went out to the big bookstore near the mall, and walked around for, like, an hour before we got coffee and stuff."

"Please tell me there was no embarrassing PDA in the café," I tease her. I find my huge, fuzzy socks with pink and black stripes and slide them on before I curl up next to Darcia.

Jess rolls her eyes. "Please." She waits a beat before she grins and says, "We made out in his car in the parking lot."

"Classy!" Dar and I say together, giggling.

"Hey, it was too late for a movie by then." Jess sniffs, but she's still smiling. There's something new in her eyes, too, a dreamy little sparkle. I haven't seen that in a long time, and I reach across the bed to pinch her foot.

"So he's a good guy, huh?"

"He's pretty awesome, if you ask me," Dar cuts in. Every trace of laughter is gone. "I know Jimmy Coes is just a freshman, but he's a lot taller than I am. And he was, like, strong. Plus, I was so surprised, I didn't even have time to yell, and then I had this gross tongue in my mouth and—"

"Oh, Dar." Jess reaches out and lays a hand on her arm. "I didn't know he really scared you."

"I think that's what got Cal's attention. He walked by, and I was staring around Jimmy's head, and I kind of . . . flapped my hands at him." She's flushed now, eyes focused on her bare feet.

"Well, I'm glad he did." I keep my voice as steady as possible. "That's totally uncool, even if Jimmy is just a kid. Attack does not equal flirt, you know?"

"Exactly." Jess is flushed, too, but I think it's pride. Even she never expected Cal to pull a white knight like that, and she expects pretty much everything from the few boys she's ever been interested in.

"Anyway." Darcia smiles up at us from beneath her lashes. They're as dark and thick as her hair. "I just hope I thanked him enough."

"You totally did," Jess assures her. "For a while last night I was actually beginning to wish he would change the subject. I mean, I don't want it going to his head."

I snort and flop back on the pillows, staring at the ancient glow-in-the-dark stars in Darcia's ceiling. They don't actually glow anymore, but I know the pattern of them by heart.

It's something to focus on instead of how hard it is to join in this conversation without bursting into tears.

A week ago, I would have been gushing about Gabriel. A week ago, I usually was gushing about Gabriel, or at least what passes for gushing with me. A week ago, I didn't think our relationship could be any more perfect.

Being wrong is a habit I'd really like to break.


Horror gets outvoted in favor of some romance thing with men in riding breeches and women in long, pale dresses, so I spend most of the movie imagining what would happen if they were being attacked by zombies. It's a decent way to pass the time, snuggled between Jess and Dar in the nest we've made of Dar's bed. There's popcorn and root beer and peanut M&M's and mini doughnuts drenched in powdered sugar, and by the time the movie's over I'm slightly nauseous in the best possible way.

"Okay, I know that look," Jess says as the credits roll, elbowing Darcia in the ribs. She sits up and stretches; white powder clings to one cheek. "Who are you thinking about? You've got a secret Mr. Darcy in your head, don't you? You do! Come on, spill."

Dar groans and rolls over, burying her face in the pillows. She grunts something unintelligible, and I help Jess roll her over again.

"Tell," I say, pressing the tip of one finger to her nose gently.

She sighs and screws her eyes shut tight, like if she can't see us, we can't see her. "Thierry Dupuis."

Jess frowns at me over Dar's closed eyes, and I mouth *French kid* as I tug one of Dar's curls. "Dar, he's adorable."

"He's the French kid," she explains to Jess when she finally sits up, as if she knew all along he's someone who wouldn't register on Jess's radar. "The one here until the end of April?"

Jess's smile is crooked and pleased. "Very nice."

"We actually talked at the party," Dar admits. "Before, you know. He plays the guitar, too."

"I wonder if the French are actually better at French kissing," Jess wonders aloud, and Dar throws a piece of popcorn at her.

Suddenly her face falls, and she and Jess exchange a

look before turning to me. Uh-oh. I can practically taste the questions in the air.

"Have you talked to Gabriel since the party?" Dar asks gently, and I try not to sigh out loud.

Instead, I just shake my head, hoping they'll get the idea I don't want to talk about it. That's never stopped Jess, of course.

"I wish I knew what you guys are actually fighting about," she says, and leans toward me, frowning. "I mean, everything was so great, and then . . ."

"Yeah, well." I shrug. My cheeks are burning, and every nerve is singing with the urge to run. I don't want to be the center of attention, not about this.

Dar's bedroom door bangs open. *Saved by the fourth grader,* I think with relief as Dex announces, "Come on! It's eleven thirty, and the ball-drop thing is starting soon!" His dark hair is slightly sweaty, shoved off his forehead in seven different directions, and someone plastered a temporary lightning-bolt tattoo in the middle of it.

"We don't want to miss that," I say, and stand up, collecting snacks as I go.

Dar bites her bottom lip, but she doesn't say anything, and Jess gets up off the bed, grabbing empty root beer bottles and teasing Dex, "Where's your broom, Harry?"

Downstairs, the living room is crowded—Davina is

home for the holidays, and Mrs. Banerjee's sister, Sophia, is visiting. The youngest of Dar's brothers, David, is already cross-legged in front of the TV in SpongeBob pajamas. He's a curly head like Darcia, and just in second grade.

"Girls, just in time for the par-tay," Mr. Banerjee says, and Darcia groans. Dion, who started seventh grade this year, lopes in, still in his jeans and a plain gray T-shirt. He doesn't really look at Jess and me. She thinks we make him nervous now.

I think he and Robin would be pretty cute together, but maybe in a couple years. Like, five. Or nine.

For a little while, it's too noisy and chaotic to even think about Gabriel. Dar's mom is passing around paper cups of sparkling grape juice, and Dex and David are singing along with the boy band in Times Square. It's so familiar and so stupidly fun, I'm happy to perch on one arm of the sofa with Dar's dad and tell him about my new camera.

At 11:58, Dar looks up from where David has her pinned on the carpet and says, "The confetti!"

I get up. "I'll get it, Dar. Be right back."

"Get the hats and stuff, too!"

I'm already halfway up the stairs but I yell back okay, and have to fumble along the wall to find the light switch.

"Hurry," Jess yells from downstairs, and I roll my eyes.

By the time I stumble into Dar's room, I can hear them downstairs, chanting, "Eight, seven, six," but as I grab the hats and noisemakers, my phone rings. It's lying on Darcia's night table, shimmying closer as it vibrates, and I can see Gabriel's name on the screen.

I drop everything and snatch it up. "Gabriel?"

"Wren." His smile is right in his voice, rounding it out full and warm. "I just wanted to tell you I love you, and happy New Year. I know we need to—"

"*Gabriel.*" I wonder if he knows tears are streaming down my cheeks. I wonder if he knew I was aching all night, missing him.

"So you're not mad," he says. I want to reach through the phone and hold on to him, breathe him in.

"Not about this," I whisper, sniffling. "But we should, you know, talk." I curl up on Darcia's bed with the phone pressed to my ear. Downstairs, everyone's shouting and cheering.

Dar and Jess come up a minute later, pushing into the room and demanding to know what happened to me. I mouth *Gabriel* at them and point to the phone. They're both grinning when they back out of the room and close the door.

# CHAPTER FIFTEEN

"NEW YEAR'S DAY IS REALLY THE PERFECT kind of day," I say, curling closer to Gabriel. I'm talking mostly to his hair at this point, and my breath must tickle because he wriggles and laughs.

"Oh yeah? Why is that?"

"Because you don't have to do anything. Nothing. No gifts, no big meals, no parades, no football, no—"

Gabriel snorts and pushes me off him to sit up. "Wren. Seriously?"

"What?" I push my own messy hair out of my eyes. I think I lost a clip at some point when we were making out before.

"The Rose Parade? College football?" He chokes out a laugh. "You have no idea what I'm talking about, do you?"

"Fine, be a boy," I say, and get up, sniffing dramatically. "In my house, there's no football."

He stands up, too, but slowly, and I realize he's inching closer. I look up at him through my lashes, ready to run.

"Does that mean you've never been . . . tackled?" he asks me, and I take off, shrieking, hoping the downstairs neighbors are either too hungover to hear us or out somewhere.

He chases me through the apartment, but there aren't many places to go, and I nearly topple over a chair when I get past him on my way out of the kitchen. I catch my sock on a splintered floorboard, snagging to an awkward stop, and just as I wrestle my bare foot out of it, he pounces.

We wind up on the floor of his bedroom, laughing and panting, him on top of me, his body a long, narrow cage.

We haven't actually talked much yet about all the many things we should talk about, but for now, I don't care.

I reach up to run my fingers through his hair and pull his head down for a kiss. He comes willingly, and I sigh as our lips touch. My mouth feels a little bruised already—

we've been kissing a *lot*—but it's totally worth it.

I'm keeping a tight leash on the magic, though, because the last thing I want is for the two of us to wind up floating off the planet while we're messing around. Besides, this—the solid, heavy feel of him stretched alongside me, the taste of his mouth, the warm weight of his hands—is just perfect.

I left Dar's this morning as soon as it seemed polite. There was the traditional big breakfast first, and then as I was leaving I called my mom to tell her where I was headed.

"Ah," she'd said, and I could picture her smile. "Have you reached a truce?"

"We're getting there," I said, hefting my duffel over one shoulder as I trudged toward Gabriel's apartment in the frigid silence of New Year's morning.

"And is Olivia home?"

"I have no idea, Mom." I rolled my eyes. "We *had* the talk, remember? More than once, if I remember right."

She'd just sighed. "Well, you're not sleeping over there tonight, so call me later, huh?"

I think I promised. It's getting harder to remember anything that happened after Gabriel opened the door and pulled me inside, kissing me for so long I was a little breathless. He was in gray sweats and a soft, faded blue

171

flannel shirt, and he smelled so good, I kept lowering my head to his shoulder and breathing in the dark, rich scent hidden in the hollow of his throat.

He rolls to the side a little bit, one leg still slung over both of mine, and traces my face with one finger. "Now you've been tackled."

"You win," I whisper, and pretend to bite at his finger as it passes over my mouth. "Touchdown."

"We should probably be talking about other things, right?" he says, but he doesn't look very eager. His hair is crazy, and his face is hot with color.

I sigh and push up on my elbows. "Probably. It would be all grown-up and mature and stuff. Dr. Phil would approve."

He snorts again, and I like the wicked glint in his eyes. "Let's definitely not do that then."

I scratch my cheek idly and tilt my head, trying not to smile. "What should we do instead?"

His grin gets just evil enough to make me giggle. "I have a couple of ideas."

Since Olivia is at a friend's for the day, we don't talk much for the rest of the afternoon. Turns out that's totally okay with both of us.

I had planned on Sunday being more of the same—me, Gabriel, kissing, then more kissing—but Jess is adamant.

"Come on, Wren." She's practically whining, which she never does, and it startles me to attention. "I want you to see what I see. Cal is so sweet, and you don't really know him."

A double date. Jess is proposing a double date, me and Gabriel, her and Cal, and it's so unbelievable, I check the readout on my phone to make sure it's actually her.

There's just one thing that stops me from saying yes immediately. Well, aside from losing the chance to spend the afternoon curled up with Gabriel, making out until we're dizzy with it. "Is Dar going to feel left out?"

"No!" She sounds positively giddy. "She and her French dude are going to be working on songs at her house this afternoon. He called her last night."

"Ooh la la," I say, and laugh, but I'm pumped. Dar moons over boys at home alone, but she rarely makes a move, and she's so shy a lot of guys just ignore her.

"So we're doing this?" Jess demands, and it's impossible to say no to that tone.

"We're doing this," I tell her, and then I stop. "What exactly *are* we doing?"

A movie, it turns out. The Rialto is donating half the ticket sales for the two afternoon shows to a fund Adam's parents set up. There are flyers up all over the lobby, thanks to Audrey, I bet.

"We should sit in the back," Gabriel whispers into

my ear as we walk into the theater, and I elbow him, giggling.

"Are there going to be explosions? I like movies where shit blows up," Cal says to Jess. He's teasing, a smirk curling up one corner of his mouth.

"Very funny." She tucks herself under his arm before turning into a row just six or seven from the back, and I watch as he kisses the top of her head. He's huge compared to her, this solid block of boy in an actual football jacket, but he's got a gooey marshmallow center I didn't expect. When he looks at her, his brown eyes go soft and sort of dreamy, like he'd run into a burning building for her and write her a poem while he was at it. It's adorable.

"He's really not bad," I whisper to Gabriel as we take our seats beside them. "I actually like him."

"And it's all about you, right?" He ducks when I try to elbow him again and grabs my hand to hold it tight. "Hey, I know what you mean. He's pretty cool."

It's hard to remember how furious and heartbroken I was just days ago when Gabriel has one arm around me in the dark theater, and he's feeding me greasy popcorn. I keep glancing sideways at Jess and Cal, too, and biting my lip to keep from grinning when I see her head on his shoulder and his fingers combing through her hair.

Even as the huge screen explodes in gunfire and a

ridiculous car chase, I'm thinking that I don't want to mess this up again.

The gray winter light is shocking when we come out of the movie theater, and I huddle deep inside my coat as I search for my gloves. Gabriel wraps his scarf around his neck, and doubles mine, tucking the ends inside the front of my jacket.

"Well, I never thought I'd see someone drive a car down subway tracks," Cal says, rubbing his hands together. He's grinning, all bright white teeth and laughter.

"I never thought I'd believe Rob Pattinson as an FBI agent." Gabriel smirks before adding, "Still not sure I do, actually."

"It's too cold to stand out here," Jess announces, scanning the street with purpose. "Let's go get hot chocolate. With extra chocolate."

"And extra hot," Cal adds, swinging an arm around her. "Bliss is on me, unless you want to go somewhere else, Wren."

"Are you kidding? Geoff gives us free stuff." I take Gabriel's hand and start walking down Broad Street, still shivering.

We're just rounding the corner onto Elm when I spot Fiona and Bay. They're coming out of Bliss hand in hand, and for a moment everything goes slow-motion, syrupy.

He glances up, recognizing me, and even from a block away I can feel the weight of his gaze. Trained on me like a laser sight, taking in everything around me, including Cal and Jess and Gabriel.

That's all it takes for my happiness, so solid and unbreakable just minutes ago, to shatter. I can practically hear it as time speeds up to normal again, and my breath stutters in my throat.

It's so stupid. I'm not cheating on Gabriel, and it's not like I've been running around knocking over convenience stores or smoking crack in some back alley. But it feels wrong that I haven't told Gabriel about them. Hell, it feels wrong that I haven't told Jess and Dar about them.

And for a split second, I wonder if it's because the only reason I hang out with them is for the magic.

That feels wrong, too.

I must have slowed down, because Gabriel is pulling me along the sidewalk and saying, "Wren? You in there?"

I swallow and nod, pasting on a smile. "Sorry. I was just trying to figure out if it's physically possible to drive a Mini Cooper through the subway while you're bleeding out of your femoral artery."

Bay and Fiona are closer now, heading toward us on the opposite side of the street, and Bay's dark eyes are following every step I take. Watching me and smiling a small, secret smile that makes the hair on the back of my neck prickle.

Fiona is nose-down in an enormous latte, completely oblivious as usual, but my heart is still pounding. Jess and Cal are laughing about the movie, and Gabriel's arm is tucked around my waist, firm and warm, and I want to blink my eyes and make something disappear—us or them, I'm not sure.

But even though he never stops staring, Bay and Fiona pass by without a word, and I'm drawing in a shuddery breath as we open the door to the café. Geoff is at the counter, and he beams at us over the heads of the people in line, and the steamy sweetness inside feels so familiar and safe, my heart finally slows down to normal.

Gabriel squeezes my hand, looking at me carefully, and I make sure my smile is bright and calm. I'm so transparent to him, it's hard to believe he hasn't seen the secrets I'm still keeping, or my guilt at having them at all.

But he hasn't opened up to me completely yet, either. Even now I can tell by his pinched expression that another headache is starting, but I know he won't say anything if I don't ask. I let him lead me up to the counter as Jess chatters about hot chocolate and chocolate croissants on top of it, but my appetite is long gone.

# CHAPTER SIXTEEN

MONDAY IS PROBABLY THE FIRST TIME EVER I'm glad to go back to school after a vacation. For once, the regular routine of it feels good, like my favorite jeans—comfortable, familiar, normal.

And if I spend one more minute with Robin moping or weeping or accidentally making flowers grow out of the dining room wallpaper, I'm going to scream.

Plus, there's Gabriel waiting for me at my locker. "Hey." He smiles and bends down to kiss me, and I stretch up on my toes to meet him. We walk to homeroom hand in hand, and snatches of conversation drift past on the current of noise in the hallway: ". . . not *believe* he said that to my face . . ." and ". . . fireworks at the dorm, isn't that weird . . ." and ". . . got a car for Christmas, seriously?" With my free hand, I touch the charms on the necklace Gabriel gave me.

"I have to work today after school," he says as we take our seats. "Sheila's got a doctor's appointment or something, so I'm going to have to run, like, right when the bell rings."

"Oh. Bummer." I let my shoulders slump, since I don't have to work till tomorrow, and I was already planning on spending the afternoon with him.

"Only till six or so. She texted me this morning." He reaches across the aisle and takes my hand. "We could do homework together tonight, though. Olivia will be working. You could meet me at the shop when I get off."

"That's not a totally sucky plan B." I grin at him, and we drop hands when Mr. Rokozny comes in, looking like every minute of his break was spent plotting either a new career path or ways to destroy us all.

It's a mostly quiet day, aside from the occasional groan from someone getting an exam back. I drift through the morning, holding on to those moments in the theater, and the day before at Gabriel's house, not paying attention at all to differential equations or French irregular conjugations.

Maybe those moments with Gabriel weren't as perfect as they could be, but for now I'll take what I can get.

I find Gabriel in the cafeteria at lunchtime, already at our usual table with a bowl of something horrifically orange and congealed, and a wilted salad.

I plop down my brown bag. "What the hell is that?"

"I'm told it's minestrone. I highly doubt it, though." He peeks into my bag. "Please tell me you have something like a Twinkie in here."

Jess shows up, waving a banana victoriously. "I *aced* my history exam."

I groan and rip open my yogurt. "You'll write to me from Harvard, right?"

Before she can say anything, the cafeteria goes weirdly quiet, and I look up to find five girls on the stage at the far end of the room. Each of them has on a black T-shirt with the words FIND ADAM in stark white letters emblazoned on the front. Audrey stands in the middle of them, holding the microphone.

"Thanks, everybody. I just wanted to say that we raised a lot of money for the Adam Fund yesterday at the Rialto, and the Palickis really appreciate every dollar." Her voice doesn't waver for a moment, and she looks so determined, so strong, she's sort of awesome. "All of it is going toward efforts to find Adam—more flyers, a website, and all the resources we need for those things. They haven't given up, and I hope you won't give up on helping them."

"We have T-shirts for sale, too," Cleo says, taking the mike when Audrey hands it to her. Her shirt has been pulled tight and tied just above her belly button. Of course. "Only seven dollars. We'll have a table in here every lunch period."

Someone behind me starts clapping, and soon the whole room erupts in applause. Audrey waves, and the other girls follow her off the stage. From a distance, they look a little like five sad black ducklings.

Jess is already checking her wallet for cash, but the rest of us go back to eating. Post-break isn't the best time to expect anyone to have money to burn, but I decide I'll buy a shirt when I get my next paycheck. I know what grief feels like, and something I've managed to bury pretty deep aches when I imagine Adam's family, trying so hard to find him.

Or what happened to him.

It's a sobering thought, and I dig into my yogurt to distract myself.

Behind us, a couple of kids sit down with their trays and insulated lunch bags. I scoot my chair in just as one of them says, "Everyone's mad, and no one knows what to do. The house looks like someone dipped it in Pepto-Bismol, and the neighbors swear they didn't see anything."

A distant alarm clangs in my head, but it's hard to hear in the cafeteria's din.

"Dude. Who could paint a whole house without being seen?" another kid asks around a mouthful of sandwich.

"Uh, that's the point." I glance over my shoulder in time to see a French fry arcing over the table. "But the neighbors are clueless."

"That's effed up," another kid says with a knowing nod, and I turn around, my spoon suspended over my plastic cup of fat-free Raspberry Cheesecake.

It doesn't mean anything. I mean, pranks are pranks, and lots of people pull them. People who aren't Bay and Fiona.

But I can hear her voice in my head, that naughty singsong, chattering about turning a block of Elm Street pink, and Bay nodding and laughing like it was the best, funniest plan in the world.

And all afternoon, I try to ignore the feeling that there just aren't a lot of people who could paint an entire house in a single night without being seen. It doesn't work very well.

★ ★ ★

"So you're all ready?" Jess asks, appearing at my locker at the end of the day. She's already in her coat, bag packed and slung neatly over one shoulder. She glances at my bag, open on the floor at my feet, frowning. "Did you remember samples?"

I close my locker and spin the dial before turning around to stare at her. "You want to give me, like, one clue what you're talking about?"

She stares right back, waiting for me to break, I guess, and finally frowns. "The yearbook meeting? Hello?"

Oh. Oh *shit*.

"You didn't," she says, eyes wide, and then her shoulders slump as she shakes her head. "You did, didn't you? You totally forgot."

I smile weakly. "Um . . ."

"God, Wren." She huffs and looks at her watch. "Look, it's not till four, right? You have time. You could go home right now and get everything together."

"Am I forgetting about some secret jet pack I'm supposed to be using? It's three fifteen now!"

Uh-oh. Her hands are on her hips now, and her foot is about to start tapping. Next thing I know, she'll be spitting out my full name like I'm really in trouble. "You can get there if you hurry. And you should, because this will look great on college applications. It's not like you do anything else."

"Hey," I manage because that stings.

"I didn't mean it like that." Her face softens. "Just . . . how could you forget?"

"I was a little busy having a nervous breakdown over Gabriel, you know," I hiss. "And not everyone is as perfect as you are, okay?"

"You know if you would stop whining and leave, you could be back on time," she says pointedly, and I growl at her until she backs up.

"Call me after," she yells from halfway down the hall, and I groan as I put my coat on.

I can't believe I forgot—on Christmas Eve I actually started putting together some photos to bring to the stupid meeting, and I'd decided I really wanted to do it. Maybe Jess isn't wrong about writing things down.

I'm still muttering to myself, trying to ignore the angry flares of power in my gut, which would love to spark out and smash something, when I get to the north door. A couple kids are still milling around, lighting cigarettes, and opening up their cell phones.

And Bay and Fiona are leaning against the bike racks, grinning at me.

My voice freezes in my throat for a moment, but no one is paying any attention to them. Or to me, for that matter. Even with Fiona perched on the railing in a bright purple coat with glittery butterflies all over it, her hair a firmly sprayed cloud of cotton candy.

"Hey there, little girl," Bay says, and I make a face at him.

"Don't be gross. Ick."

"Come play with us," Fiona says, hopping off the bike rack and skipping forward to grab my hand. "It's been days and days since we've seen you!"

"I can't," I say, taking my hand back quickly. "I have this thing, and I have to—"

"So we'll drop you off," Bay says easily, standing up. "I've got the car, come on."

A car. That's actually handy. I consider for a minute, flapping my hand at Fiona when she dances around me like a deranged firefly. "Okay, let's go."

She whoops and skips toward the parking lot with Bay and me trailing behind her. "Is she on a sugar high every day?" I ask, only half kidding.

"I think she was born on one." He laughs and points his keys at a red Jetta. It beeps and Fiona opens the door, climbing in the back.

"You get shotgun," she yells from inside, and I can't help smiling, even though I'm dying to know if they were responsible for the Pepto-Bismol nightmare house. For once, I wish I had Gabriel's power instead of my own.

"Okay, I live across town, just past the—"

"Later," Bay says as he starts the engine. The doors lock automatically, and I jump. "We have a little errand we could use your help with first."

"Bay, no," I protest, my heart thumping again. He pulls out of the lot smoothly, but he takes the turns way faster than he should. Then again, he doesn't crash, so what do I know? I fasten my seat belt anyway. "I have to get home so I can pick up my camera. There's a yearbook meeting I need to—"

"Yearbook?" Fiona groans dramatically. "This is going to be much more fun, I promise you." She unwraps a piece of gum, and suddenly the car smells like ripe strawberries.

"Well, you can have your fun without me," I tell her firmly, even though I'm staring at the side of Bay's face. "I need to go home, so if you just pull over, I'll get out here." We're near the traffic circle, and Bay veers right instead of left. "Bay, come on."

"Shhh, watch." He points out the windshield, and I watch as the red light up ahead suddenly turns green. The opposing traffic screeches to a halt, and I wonder if their green lights even went to yellow or just blinked right to red.

Fiona hoots. I slap my hand over my mouth, shocked. I can't believe he just did that, and I really can't believe I didn't hear the shrieking metal sound of cars crashing.

"Bay, what the fuck?" I manage when my heart stops pounding in my throat.

"Calm down," he says easily, waving a hand at me. "Nothing happened."

"But . . ."

"Wren, loosen up, sweetie." Fiona hands me a piece of gum, like it's the answer to all my problems. "He's a good driver."

My mouth is hanging open, but I can't make any more sounds come out. I knew they liked to "play," but I never pictured anything dangerous. Anything so reckless that innocent people could have been hurt.

Bay glances at me and reaches over to pat my shoulder. "I'll be good. Now relax, huh? We have important business to take care of here."

My house and my camera and the yearbook meeting are fading into the distance with every block, and unless I can figure out how to, like, teleport in the next five minutes, I'm stuck.

Furious and horrified and stuck. I grit my teeth and pretend to relax into my seat. If nothing else, I can see for myself how far they're willing to go, even if I can't get a definitive answer about the pink house. And I'm beginning to think that I should know what they're capable of before I wind up doing something I really don't want to do.

Well, something *else* anyway.

"I thought we were off to have 'fun,'" I say. It's not totally possible to keep the sarcasm out of my tone, but I give it a shot.

"Whoever said business couldn't be mixed with pleasure was wrong," Fiona chirps, and I pretend to smile while I hang on for the ride.

# CHAPTER SEVENTEEN

"WHERE WERE YOU?" ARE THE FIRST WORDS out of Gabriel's mouth when he opens the door to his apartment later that evening. It's after seven, and he's already changed into his oldest jeans and a threadbare T-shirt the color of ripe olives. His feet are bare—it's always warmer up on the third floor than it needs to be, even in January. "I waited at the shop till six thirty."

For a minute I just hang my head. I'm tired and out of breath, since I was trying to hurry after Bay dropped me in town.

I walk past him into the living room, shedding my backpack and peeling off my coat as I go. I'm craving coffee or even tea, anything hot, but it doesn't seem like the time to ask.

"Wren?"

I realize I haven't answered him yet, and I turn around slowly, scrambling to say something. "I ran into some people, and I lost track of time."

His face is too blank, but his eyes are focused on me like lasers, and I swallow hard. It feels like a lie.

Especially since I don't really want to tell him what I was doing, not anymore. We ended up at a swim meet at the community college, where a girl who was competing had apparently called Fiona a slut sometime in the past few days. I stopped watching the mischief they were causing from the top of the bleachers after her straps tore, and she wound up flashing the entire pool.

"You didn't call." Gabriel turns around to walk into the kitchen then. His shoulders are set too stiffly, as if he's carrying something heavy and awful on them. He looks the way he does when a headache is starting.

Crap.

I follow him into the kitchen, where he's grabbing a soda out of the fridge. There's a bag on the table from Cosimo's, and the bottom is shiny with grease. I can smell meatballs and cheese—my favorite sandwich.

"I'm sorry," I say, coming up behind him to run a

hand over his back. "I wasn't thinking."

He turns around, shutting the fridge with his hip. "Who did you run into?"

"Just some friends." I shrug and open the bag. "Do you want to eat? Or do you want me to go home?"

He sets the can of soda on the table with a bang. It's a diet, for me. "You know what? I don't want you to be here if you don't want to be. Fuck."

He pushes past me to walk out of the room, and I stumble against the table. He almost never swears, and for a minute all I can think to do is leave. But I'm not doing that anymore; I promised myself. Running away never works. Running away makes you the worst kind of coward, unless someone is actually chasing you with, like, a machete. I'm not even going to run from Bay and Fiona anymore.

But I am going to tell them it's over, whatever this weird friendship thing is. As soon as I can figure out how.

So I straighten up and walk back into the living room, where Gabriel's sitting with his elbows propped on his knees, his head hanging low over his chest.

"I'm here, Gabriel. I wouldn't be if I didn't want to be. You should know that." I move a couple of yoga magazines and an empty mug to sit on the coffee table in front of him. "Without looking in my head."

His head snaps up, eyes flashing. "I told you I don't do that anymore."

"I know." I push my knee toward his, bumping it. "But when you don't, it seems like you're never really sure of me."

"I'm just pissed off." He sits back, breaking even that casual contact. "You said you would meet me at work, and you didn't."

"God, I said I'm sorry, and I am!" I tilt my head back but the ceiling is only a blank white square. "I was just late, Gabriel." I figure it's a good thing he clearly forgot about the yearbook meeting, or I'd probably get chided for missing that, too.

His eyes are still hot, burning into me. "And you won't tell me who you were with."

The anger in his eyes lights up my own, a nasty flame. "Is this some ridiculous jealous-boyfriend thing? Because I really think you know me better than that."

It's his turn to address the ceiling, shaking his head as he does. "I know you're not cheating on me. But I can't help wondering why you won't say where you were."

I'm hungry and tired, and I stand up, trembling. "Who says you get to know everything about me, Gabriel? You've already got the double secret password into my brain, even if you don't use it anymore. And if you want a list of all the things you won't tell *me*, you can get me a ream of paper because we're going to be here all night."

The words explode into the air like shrapnel, and Gabriel actually flinches. I sit down abruptly, still breathing hard, still angry, but I can't look at him. I don't know what I'll see in his eyes. I didn't even mean to say that.

"What haven't I told you?" he says after a silence that goes on way too long. "What do you want to know?"

"Everything! You know everything about me, and you did a long time before I was ready to tell you." I lift my head to face him, and this time he looks away.

The living room is suddenly too small, suffocating, and I want to blast a hole through it to let the winter night in. But I don't really want to blast a hole through Gabriel's secrets—I want him to open himself up and show me who he is.

As quickly as it flared, my frustration sputters out. "I don't want to fight. But I do have questions. There's a lot of stuff I don't know about you, stuff it seems like a girlfriend *should* know, and . . . it hurts."

He leans into me, sturdy and solid, and nods. "Okay. So ask."

I wasn't expecting that.

But I can't start with the big ones—why won't you talk about your dad, what makes you look so sad sometimes, why do you worry so much about me?

To buy time, I reach down to take off my boots and then turn sideways on the couch, cross-legged, so I can look at him. "How many places have you lived?"

He lets out a soft, weary breath. "Wow. Um, let me think." He's quiet for a while, eyes focused on something I can't see. "Since I was born? Uh, fourteen, unless I'm forgetting something."

I can only blink, my mouth wide open. He's only seventeen now. "Um. Oh."

"Yeah." He turns sideways, too, so we're face-to-face. "My favorite, aside from here, was this little town in northern California, on the coast. You could smell the ocean in everything."

"How old were you then?"

"Eight. It was pretty cool." His smile is tight, an effort.

I plunge on anyway. How old he was when his mom died, what she died of, what he wanted to be when he grew up back when he was in kindergarten, and the name of the first girl he ever kissed and when. He tells me everything—I can't help grinning when he says he wanted to be a ninja—but he keeps it simple, one or two words where I want dozens, details, memories. It's sort of like hearing *The Lord of the Rings* is about a piece of jewelry and some short people.

I'm running out of things to ask, and I'm so hungry I'm beginning to feel a little dizzy. That's when Gabriel turns the tables, of course.

"So, quid pro quo. Where were you this afternoon?"

I groan. "Did you take Latin in one of your many other schools?"

"Wren." He leans in and rests his forehead against mine. The urge to climb into his lap and kiss him until he shuts up is pretty tempting, but fair is fair, I guess. It's not like I can keep Fiona and Bay from him forever.

Well, I could. But I shouldn't, and I shouldn't want to. If he's supposed to be honest with me, then I owe him the same courtesy.

But before I can find my voice, Christmas night, and his horror at my little snow show, flashes through my mind. I take a deep breath.

"I met some kids," I say, pulling back far enough to look him in the eye. "And they're . . . like me. They have power, too."

His face changes so fast, I jerk. For one brief moment, all of his walls come down and panic flashes raw pewter in his eyes.

"It's fine," I say quickly, grabbing his hand and squeezing it. I want to keep him here, listening, not off

195

in his imagination picturing disaster. "They're just . . . you know, kids. And I figured maybe they would know some things about the magic that I don't."

He narrows his eyes. "How did you find them?"

*No more lying,* I tell myself firmly. But my voice comes out barely a whisper. "They . . . saw me. Doing some stuff."

*"Wren."*

"Look, I know, okay?" I hold his hand tighter, as if he can feel the truth in my touch. "And we've hung out some."

He must hear the hesitation in my tone, because his eyes narrow again, looking into me. Not like that, just like . . . a concerned boyfriend. I manage a half smile.

"But they're reckless."

"You know, you have a brilliant career as a detective ahead of you." I'm trying to play it casual, laugh it off, but he's not done.

"Tell me."

"Look, they're sort of . . . well, *reckless* is a good word. They like to 'play,' as they call it. And I don't really want to hang out with them anymore, not after today, so—"

"What did they do?"

I like him cutting me off about as much as I like Bay doing it, and I give him a good angry glare to prove it.

"Nothing illegal. I mean, they're not committing murder or something. Seriously, they're harmless, just . . . pranky."

He lifts an eyebrow. "Pranky? Really?"

I smack his arm. "You know what I mean."

"No, I really don't. I want to meet them, Wren."

I gape. "But . . . I told you I don't even want to hang out with them anymore. They're not criminals, Gabriel, just sort of stupid and immature."

And hurtful and a little bit malicious. But I'm not going to say that.

"And I just want to see for myself, okay?" He leans closer to run his hand over my cheek, into my hair. "People like that get nasty, believe me. I just . . . want to make sure they're not going to fuck with you."

I sigh. He looks so gentle, so gorgeous and sweet, and he's like a huge, stubborn, immovable brick wall when he wants to be.

"Okay. But you asked."

"I could get used to this," I say as I climb into Olivia's car on Friday night. "Walking is for suckers."

Gabriel snorts and turns the car on, waiting as it wheezes into gear. "Don't hold your breath. This thing is dying in stages. I think the engine is held together with rubber bands."

"Exciting," I say brightly, but I make sure to fasten my seat belt.

I don't want anything to ruin tonight, and so far everything is going according to plan. Bay suggested a party out at Summerhill, Olivia was willing to walk down to the bar and back for work so Gabriel could use the car, and the snow that has been threatening for days is still a distant bank of gloom on the horizon.

Gabriel sort of looks like we're headed to a hanging instead of a party, though.

"We don't have to stay long," I tell him as he pulls the car onto the street. My seat vibrates as the engine chugs along.

He shrugs. "I know."

Since the radio died a few weeks ago and he doesn't seem to be in the mood for conversation, either, we ride the rest of the way in silence.

Classes don't start again at Summerhill until next week, so the campus is mostly empty, dark under its canopy of bare branches. But inside O'Keefe Hall, the student lounge upstairs is like a pounding heart in the sleeping dorm.

I don't see Bay and Fiona right away, and Gabriel slings an arm around my shoulders once we're inside, as if he's going to lose me in the crush. But there aren't really that many people in the long room—maybe thirty, sprawled on industrial-issue sofas or perched in the deep window seats. It's dark, the room lit only by an assortment of lava lamps and string after string of colored Christmas lights.

"Wren?"

I turn around from inspecting the beer and soda in the cooler along one wall to see Jude. "Hey!"

She doesn't look happy to see me, and she's giving Gabriel the same vaguely disturbed little frown. "What are you doing here?"

"Party crashing." I grin. "No, Bay mentioned it, and I wanted him to meet Gabriel." That's a white lie I can rationalize under the circumstances. "Gabriel, this is Jude. She's a junior here."

"Hi." Gabriel sticks his hand out, and even though Jude seems surprised by the show of manners, she shakes it.

"Nice to meet you. Um, I'm not sure Bay's even here. . . ." She twists her head to scan the room just as Fiona pops up behind her back, whispering, "Boo."

"But Fiona is," Jude says with a tight smile. "Well. Have a good time." She's gone before Fiona can do more than leave a bright red lip print on her cheek.

"Wee barista!" Fiona cries, and leans in to hug me, a little too hard. She's in her rabbit fur jacket again, over black skinny jeans and a white-and-black-striped top, complete with a red beret and huge, white fur boots. She looks sort of like a castoff snow bunny by way of 1950s Paris. "I'm so glad you came! And who is this very yummy tall person with you?"

Okay, that needs to stop right now. I take a step between them. "This is Gabriel. My boyfriend. Gabriel, this is Fiona."

Fiona smirks and actually bats her lashes, and I stomp on the urge to cough up a hairball. All over her. She catches me glaring. "Just being friendly, Wren. Tick tick boom."

"Nice to meet you, Fiona." Gabriel sounds like it's anything but, and he slides his arm around my waist, fingers digging into my hip to pull me back against him.

Oh, this is going well so far.

"Does Gabriel . . . play?" Fiona is nothing if not predictable, and about as subtle as a hurricane. She's still examining him like he's some rare, possibly dangerous species, and for a moment her bright white nails look a little too much like claws.

"No," Gabriel says. The ice in his voice is thick. "I don't."

"Shame."

Before I can say anything else, she flutters off, batting

at low-hanging lights as she goes.

"Is she wearing a costume?" Gabriel mutters, and I elbow him.

Across the room, a girl with a sheet of black satin hair climbs up on a low table, and someone else turns the music up. In the near darkness, I can just make out her mouth moving before she starts to dance, and behind me Gabriel shifts uneasily.

It's sinuous, all lazy *S* curves as she moves, but the dance isn't the show—it's her skin, bare arms under a sleeveless top that just grazes her stomach, and a short skirt. She's literally a human glow stick, colored light shifting and pulsing magically under her skin as she moves, and for a minute I can't look away.

Until I see Bay, just behind her, watching with his head tilted to one side and a red cup in one hand. Something about the way he's looking at her is wrong, as if he's not just delighted but proud.

He sees me a moment later, and I straighten up as he crosses the room, pushing through a couple of kids who have gotten up to dance, too. My blood is racing, spurred by the noise and the light. Just that, I tell myself. Not nerves. Definitely not nerves.

"You came," Bay says, and drops into an empty chair beside me, one leg slung over an arm. As if he's the king, and we're commoners, peasants, come seeking an audience.

"Did you think we wouldn't?" I ask him, and grab his cup to sniff it. Something sharply alcoholic tickles my nose.

Instead of answering me, he says, "Who's this?"

"This is Gabriel." I glance over my shoulder, and my heart sinks. Gabriel's features are pinched in what looks like the start of another headache.

"Gabriel looks like he wants to be elsewhere." Bay takes his cup back and drinks from it slowly, watching me over the rim.

"I think he has a headache." I put my arm around Gabriel's waist, hoping it doesn't look like I'm propping him up, even though I'm pretty sure I am. It's never been this bad before.

"That's not much of a welcome," he says with effort.

"Hey, I call 'em like I see 'em." Bay pats his knee when Fiona reappears with her own red cup, but she squints at Gabriel instead.

"You look like shit. Are you okay?"

"Maybe some water?" I tell her, and she heads off. Her rabbit fur is gone, and in its place is the eye-watering scent of whatever perfume she put on.

"Wren was telling me about . . . about what you all can

do," Gabriel manages, and I wish there was somewhere for him to sit other than the floor. He's trying so hard to act normal, but I can tell the headache is slicing through him in angry arcs.

"Wren's a natural." Bay hasn't taken his eyes off Gabriel. "She didn't mention anything about you, though."

The words sound wrong in his mouth, but Gabriel ignores them. "Power is something that should be respected," he says instead. He's still trembling, but he's standing up a little straighter. Facing off, I think, and this is exactly what I didn't want to happen.

"Believe me, I respect her just fine." Bay stands up, crumpling his red cup. It turns to shiny red confetti as it falls to the floor. He nods at me. "Wren."

"Damn it," I mutter, and turn around just as Gabriel blinks, like he's startled, and then puts his hand to his head.

"Hey!" I grab his other hand. "Gabriel, what is it?"

"Let's get out of here," he whispers, eyes focused somewhere over my left shoulder.

For once, I don't argue with him.

# CHAPTER EIGHTEEN

PLATES AND MUGS ARE FLOATING IN MIDAIR when I walk into the kitchen the next morning, a surreal Ferris wheel of china.

I blink and take a step backward. After a night's sleep twisted in uneasy dreams, I'm not sure any of it is real until I see Robin on the other side of the room, leaning against the pantry door.

"What are you doing?"

One plate swoops higher before crashing, and Robin huffs. She's still in her pajamas, her hair scooped into a loose ponytail. "You jerk!"

"Me?" I grab another plate and a mug out of the air

and set them carefully on the table. "I don't remember telling you to levitate the dishes." I snatch at a few more, stepping around the jagged, white shards of the broken plate on the floor.

"You broke my concentration."

I roll my eyes. "Yeah, well, you apparently broke your brain. Mom'll kill you if she sees this."

"She's at work." Robin snags the last plate from where it hovers over the table, and stacks it with the others. "And it's none of your business."

I wish that were true. I wish it so hard right now, it hurts my head. I can't leave her alone to play sorcerer's apprentice, especially not with our freaking dishes, but I don't have time to babysit.

Not for Robin, anyway.

Gabriel was in such pain last night, and I was so terrified, I was shaking. I was also the one to drive us home, and if I never get behind the wheel of Olivia's Beetle again, it will be too soon. Gabriel was sweating and trembling by the time I got the door open, and he stumbled directly into his bedroom. I took off his shoes and wrestled him out of his coat before I found him some Excedrin and poured a big glass of water, and he was asleep not long afterward, fully dressed. I had to grab a quilt out of the hall closet to put over him before I left.

I need to be there with him. Not here on brat duty with a rebellious Sabrina.

"Look, I don't know what crawled up your—" I cut myself off just in time, choking back the word. "Into your head," I say instead, and Robin smirks. "You know Mom would not be okay with this, so don't expect me to cover for you if you wind up breaking everything."

"Why not?" She stands up, and for the first time I realize my little sister isn't so little anymore. I have only two inches on her, maybe less, and she's cheating anyway, lengthening her spine and arching her feet. "Mom could put them all back together. So could you. And so can I, once I figure it out."

I push past Robin to get to the coffeemaker, where Mom managed to leave at least one cup before she left. It looks a little like mud when I pour it into a mug, but I don't care.

"It's not a game, Robin. And you know we don't use magic like that."

"Yes, you do!" Robin protests. "Mom used to do it all the time, even if she pretended we didn't know! And I thought when everything changed in the fall, maybe someone would finally explain everything to me, maybe someone would *help* me."

I put my cup down on the counter. All her bravado

is gone. The girl standing in the middle of the kitchen in her puppy dog pajama pants and pink T-shirt is just a kid again, biting her bottom lip viciously so she won't cry. And superimposed there, wavering like a ghost, is myself at her age, hair wilder and shorter, but otherwise just as furious and just as confused.

The magic I've finally learned to control isn't only mine, but I don't want her to have it, not yet. I just can't decide if it's the weight I don't want her to carry, or the tingling buzz of freedom and power that comes with using it.

"Binny . . ."

"Don't call me that." She scrapes a chair away from the table and sinks into it.

I take a deep breath. "Robin. I'm sorry, okay? It's just . . . it's been so busy, with the holidays and Gabriel and all. But it's not a good idea for you to do this stuff on your own. You don't know what could happen. You . . . you don't know what you're doing."

"Because no one will explain it!" she yells, whirling around to face me. Her ruddy cheeks shine with tears. "I don't know anything! Because no one will *tell* me! I don't even get to talk to my own dad because *you* don't want to!"

The panes in the cabinet doors over the stove burst,

raining glass, and she flings herself out of the room to pound up the stairs.

Perfect.

I pick my way across the floor to finish my coffee, and consider waving the mess away with magic. It doesn't feel like punishment enough, though, and when I set my empty mug in the sink, I get the broom.

Gabriel's still asleep when I call, and Olivia is worried. "No one in our family has ever had headaches like this," she says. "Do migraines just come out of nowhere?"

I don't know what to say to that. When I hang up, I close my eyes, picturing his face, still strained, his eyes shut tight, as if he was trying not to see something.

Even a hot shower doesn't wash away the chill of worry.

There is one thing I can do, though.

I shut myself in my room with a soda and my phone, and text Bay: WHAT WAS UP LAST NIGHT?

An hour later, I try Fiona, leave them both voice mails, and text Bay again, and nothing. Now I'm pissed. It's not surprising that Fiona was acting like a bitchy elf, and flirting on top of it, but I don't get what Bay's problem was, and I don't like it. It wasn't even my idea to go to the stupid party, but Bay doesn't know that. Doesn't know that I had decided I was done with them long before last night. And if I hadn't been freaked out by Gabriel's headache, I would have confronted him then and there. Just the thought of him, smug and smiling that mysterious smile as he crumpled his cup, is enough to make me want to break some glass.

Instead, I bang around in the kitchen, making tomato soup and grilled cheese sandwiches, and take some on a tray up to Robin. She doesn't answer when I knock, but when I go back into my room I hear the telltale creak of her door opening. She may hate me at the moment, but she never refuses her favorite lunch.

With her not starving and hopefully occupied for a little while in something other than blowing up the house, I settle on my bed with half a grilled cheese on a plate. If Bay and Fiona are ignoring me, maybe there's one person who won't.

And maybe my magic is good for something other than fun.

I wipe greasy fingers on my jeans before setting my phone down on the bed in front of me. I don't know Jude's number—I don't even know her last name—but if I'm lucky, that's not going to stop me.

I lay my hands on the phone, wondering what the hell I think I'm doing. I'm not Gabriel, after all. I frown and close my eyes, concentrating on Jude's apartment, on Jude, on the phone I saw lying on her kitchen counter the day I was there. I let my power curl out slowly from my center, tentative fingers winding into the air and searching, and in less than a minute I feel my phone vibrating.

It's dialing.

I pick it up and swallow hard. What am I supposed to say? Why was Bay such an asshole last night? Why do you seem worried all the time? Why do you look at me like the big bad wolf is right over my shoulder?

Four rings, and Jude answers with the same cautious "Hello?" I always give an unfamiliar number.

"Jude?" My stupid heart is pounding.

"Um, yeah. Who is this?"

"It's Wren. From last night? And that one other time, in—"

"Wren. Right." She's silent for a moment after that, and I close my eyes, praying she doesn't hang up. "Um, what's up?"

Thank God. "Look, I know we don't know each other, like, at all. But . . ." Suddenly I have no idea what to say, or what I think she can help me with. I don't know anything about her but how unhappy she's looked the two times I've met her, and the fact that she knows Bay and Fiona, too.

She startles me out of my thoughts when she says, "Is your boyfriend okay?"

"Oh. Um, yeah, I think so." I didn't realize she was

even around when the pain started, or that she saw us leave. "He's been getting these headaches lately. It's sort of messed up."

"Yeah." She goes quiet again, and I wince. *Think,* I tell myself.

"Look, Bay was being really weird last night, and I don't . . . I mean, is he usually like that? We've been hanging out, not that much, I guess, but still, and he was cool at first, but I'm not totally comfortable with it anymore, and . . ." It's too fast, a jumble of words trailing off like a limp string, but it's out now.

The silence is huge, a gulf of nothing that I'm trying not to fill with crazy thoughts. When Jude finally says something, I nearly drop the phone.

"Look, Wren, Bay is . . . Bay is just a little off." It sounds like an understatement the way she says it. It's unsettling how easily I can picture her face, that shifting worry in her eyes. "But you've got your boyfriend and all, you know?"

"One thing doesn't have anything to do with the other," I tell her. "I wanted Bay to help me explore what I can do, not take me to a movie."

"Well, I don't know if . . ." I can hear her swallowing. "I don't know if he wants that. So. Maybe just let it go, huh?"

"Bay's the one who approached *me*." I swear I can feel

her edging away from the conversation even as I speak. "He's the one who wanted to see what I can do, not the other way around. And if he's going to be all weird and jealous, I mean, I thought he was with Fiona anyway." Sort of. It's actually hard to tell, but I've said it now.

And more than anything I hate that this might be some ridiculous testosterone match, even if my suspicion is that it's more.

"Bay is . . . not everything he says he is." Jude's choice of words is too vague, and she's not even answering my question. "Look, I have to go," she continues before I can reply. "I'm sorry, Wren, but just . . . just be careful."

She hangs up before I can ask her what I'm supposed to be careful about, and I stop short of throwing my phone across the room in frustration.

Mari's willing to come over when I call her a little while later. "Just pretend you're here to, I don't know, use the kitchen or something. If Robin thinks you're babysitting, she's going to freak again."

She shows up just a half hour later, with a tote bag full of construction-paper letters to cut out for her class. "Poor noodle," Mari says, glancing up at the second floor with a frown. "A lot of it's probably hormones on top of everything else."

I groan as I grab my coat off the rack and shrug it on. My little sister's initiation into womanhood is not something I want to think about today or any day.

"Yeah, well. Anyway, Mom should be home soon. I'll be at Gabriel's."

He was awake when I called the second time, although he sounded like a worn-out tape of himself, scratchy and faded. I head face-first into the wind and nearly run the last block, panting as I climb the stairs to his apartment.

Olivia is already gone, working again tonight, and Gabriel answers the door in a pair of gray sweatpants I've never seen before. They hang off his narrow hips under a plain, white T-shirt and his blue hoodie, and he doesn't look entirely steady on his feet.

"Have you eaten?" I ask him as I throw my coat on the nearest chair.

"No food. Ugh." It's almost a grunt, and I follow him to the couch. He sits down too carefully.

"Has this ever happened before?" I take off my boots and edge toward him slowly. I want to curl up around him, soothe away the creases of pain in his forehead, but I don't know if he wants to be touched. For the first time, he looks breakable.

"The headaches?" He backs away, but only far enough to lie down, putting his head in my lap. I touch his hair gently, combing my fingers through it. It's sweat-damp, silky.

"Well, yeah." I smile as he rolls to his side, his cheek against my thigh. "I have seen you eat before."

"Not until a few weeks ago. I mean, not like this."

"This one was really bad." I slow my hand, stroking all the way from his head down his nape to his shoulder. "I thought you were going to pass out for a minute."

"I'm aware."

"Hey, if you can worry, so can I." I wish I could see his face, but he seems comfortable, fitted against me and the back of the sofa. "Did something happen?"

He doesn't answer for so long, I wonder if he's asleep. Finally he says, "I saw something, Wren."

Okay. I mean, I figured that much. "Something . . . bad? What do you mean?"

Under my hand, his shoulder tenses. "I got a glimpse inside Bay, accidentally."

My hand has stopped moving, and I realize I'm holding my breath. I release it slowly. "What did you pick up?"

There's only one light on in the room, a lamp on the table in the corner, and the soft gold glow throws his face into shadow. In the dim light, the hair falling over his forehead looks like a painted brushstroke.

"Gabriel, please. Tell me."

"I'm trying." He holds a hand up when I groan. "Look, I know. Just . . . go easy, huh? My head feels like the wreckage after an explosion."

It's the most he's said since I got here, so I give him a minute and spend it stroking his back. Finally he looks up again.

He sits up, resting his head against the sofa. "It was just flashes, a lot vaguer than when I saw inside you the first time."

I move closer, splaying my hand lightly over his chest. His heartbeat is a steady thump behind his ribs. "So what did you see?"

"I don't know." He shrugs. "There was a butterfly or something, and everything was sort of spinning, but someone was screaming and there was . . ." He trails off and looks at me, gaze as steady now as the beat of his heart. "Wren, I think there was something about blood."

I inch closer, and he opens his arm to gather me into the circle of it. Fiona loves butterflies—she was making them that day at Jude's, and she showed up the other day in her coat of purple wings. "But why would it be so . . . obscure? What does it mean?"

"It's not always clear, you know. And maybe it's because he was drinking?" His fingers scratch through my hair gently. "But I don't like what I saw. That I felt something like blood and violence inside your . . . friend."

It's not like I hadn't made that connection. Maybe if I change the subject . . . "Do you want some tea?" I'm already getting up and heading into the kitchen.

"No," he calls. I hear his footsteps, a little slower than usual, and then he's standing beside me as I lean into the fridge, looking for I don't even know what. "Wren, look. Maybe I'm wrong, but I got a bad vibe from Bay. Really bad."

"And you have nothing to say about Fiona? No bad vibe for the pretty girl, huh?" I try to make it a joke, but it doesn't really work.

"There's nothing there." He shrugs. "She's like a blank space in the room. It's all just . . . playing dress-up."

"Yeah, well. Whatever. I'm done with them, okay?" I walk past him and straight to the sofa, where I grab my boots.

"Wren, come on." He sits down next to me. "It's not like that. But you just assume that people are good. They're *not*, Wren, not all of them. Some people are dangerous, and you don't know Bay, or what he's like, and doing magic with him . . ."

The words are choked out, and I don't know if he's still in pain or really as disturbed as he seems.

"Just forget it, okay?" I lean over and grab my other Doc. "I learned my lesson with Danny, believe me, and I'm not about to do anything 'dangerous.' This is part of me, Gabriel. You can't make it go away."

"Wren, you're not listening—"

I wrench away from his hand when he touches my shoulder and walk away to grab my coat. "No, you aren't. I keep trying to tell you, and you just don't hear me. This is me, Gabriel. This magic, this power—it's what I am. Maybe I made some wrong choices hanging out with them, but I told you, I'm done."

I leave him standing in the shadowed living room, alone.

I'm a guilty, awful liar anyway, and I'm taking it out on him. I know he's only worried, but I hate having to face that I chose to be with people who might have done horrible things. Not just pranks, not just reckless fun, but dangerous things.

I thought I knew myself better than that by now, and I walk home wondering what else I've been wrong about.

# CHAPTER NINETEEN

"SERIOUSLY, MRS. LATTIMER, I'M PANCAKED out."

Jess's mom lifts one perfectly manicured brow. "No such thing. Your metabolism doesn't hate you yet." She piles two more fluffy pancakes on my plate and turns to Darcia.

"My metabolism doesn't hate me, either?" Darcia says, and holds up her plate for more.

Perched on a stool at the end of the breakfast bar, Jess shudders. "She's like a food pusher."

"You did go a little crazy, hon," Mr. Lattimer says, snagging a pancake off the plate in the middle of the counter and eating it with his fingers. He's not wrong; there's fruit salad, scrambled eggs, bacon, and banana pancakes with strawberry butter.

"So sue me." She shrugs and scrapes her own plate into the garbage. "I had a sudden urge to be domestic."

"You mean you were possessed by Betty Crocker," Jess corrects her, and her dad laughs as he wanders away.

It's a good way to spend a Sunday morning, especially after the unrelenting suckitude that was yesterday. I almost wish I had to work at the café later, just to avoid sitting home brooding, but Bliss has been slow in the post-holiday lull. I roll up a pancake and swipe it through a lump of strawberry butter before taking a bite, and find Jess staring at me.

"What?"

She shudders again, and her mother pulls her hair smartly with a "tsk" before she takes a giant mug of coffee and wanders out to the family room.

Dar lets her fork clatter to her plate as soon as Mrs. Lattimer is gone, and sits up straight. "Guess what?"

"Uh-oh," Jess says, but she smiles and leans over the counter. "What?"

She's bouncing, biting her bottom lip to keep her grin from splitting open her face. "There's a showcase at the Book Barn in a week, and I got invited to play!"

"No way! For real?"

"Absolutely real," Dar says right before her shoulders slump. "I'm terrified."

"You're going to be awesome," Jess says, and slides down to come around the counter and hug her. "And you're going to have so many fans there, everyone's going to be like, who's that girl, she must be famous, she must have a record deal." She simply nods when Dar groans and pushes her away.

"What night is it?" I ask her, wiping my fingers on my jeans when I can't find my napkin. I open my mouth again, about to say something about making sure Gabriel has off from work, too, and just as quickly shut it again. Maybe that's not my problem anymore.

"A week from . . . wow, last Friday night." Dar slumps a little farther, and her curls hang over her face. "This is such a bad idea."

"It is not!" Jess thumps her on the back. "You play guitar like . . . someone really awesome. Are you singing original songs?"

Dar nods, all pink embarrassment and chocolate-brown eyes, wide with terror.

It's sort of amazing—the Book Barn is mostly a bookstore, but it's café competition now, too, since they expanded to open a coffee section and a place for live music. They're pretty picky about who plays there, unlike the coffeehouse way out by Summerhill. Over there it seems like the management is always dragging out some basement-dwelling relative with a ukulele.

I'm so proud of her, but I can't help the bite of jealousy. Darcia can show the world what she can do, and if the world has any sense, they'll love her. I can't show anyone what I can do.

Jess claps her hands, startling me out of my thoughts. "Oooh! Is your friend coming?"

Dar nods, but manages to frown at Jess, too. "His name is Thierry."

"You and Gabriel will be there, of course," Jess says, and I can tell she's already mentally planning the evening, using the giant clipboard in her head. She probably knows what she's going to wear.

"I'll definitely be there," I say, and gaze down into my coffee. It's almost empty, a milky film clinging to the sides of the mug.

"Shouldn't that be a 'we'?" Dar asks carefully.

"Might be." I shrug. "Might not."

"What happened now?" Jess demands, and spins my stool around without warning. My mug slides out of my hand, sloshing the remains of the coffee. "I thought you guys were all made up."

"It's complicated."

"Spill," Dar says gently, and pats my thigh. I glare at her, and she pulls her hand back quickly.

I'm not sure what to say. I can't say that I'm the one who overreacted last night without explaining what I was overreacting about. But there is something else that bothers me. "I don't like to compare him to Danny, you know? I mean, they're totally different, and that's a good thing."

"Agreed," Jess says. "Both hotties, though. It's a little infuriating, actually."

I glare at her, too, and she grins. "I'm just saying."

"Yeah, well, relative hotness aside, it's just . . . Gabriel's harder to figure out than Danny was."

"What do you mean?" Dar props her chin on her hands, frowning.

"I knew so much about Danny just because we both grew up here, you know?" I spin back toward the counter before I remember my coffee is nearly gone. "Same frame of reference or whatever. And even if we hadn't, Danny just, like, spilled stuff all over you. His favorite song—that day—why he liked his pizza with extra cheese, why cavemen would beat astronauts, anything."

"He thought cavemen would beat astronauts?" Jess says.

This time I thwap her shoulder. "The point is, Danny was like . . . an exclamation point. He was right there, telling you everything. Gabriel is a question mark. A really smart, good-looking question mark, but he doesn't give anything away."

"You know how much he likes you," Dar offers softly.

I look at my lap, the faint pen mark on one thigh where I was doodling during history. "Sometimes that's not really enough."

In my pocket, my phone trills, and I pull it out to glance at the screen. I don't feel like talking to Gabriel yet. But it's not him; it's Bay.

I slide off my stool and walk out of the room, flipping it open. "Hey. A little late, aren't you?"

"Late?" It sounds like he's outside—I can hear the rushing hum of traffic in the background.

"I called you yesterday. I texted, too, more than once. And it's not yesterday anymore." I go into the downstairs half bath and shut the door.

"I was hungover." He laughs. "I can make it up to you, though."

I'm not particularly interested in him apologizing to me. But I want to prove to myself that I can handle whatever he throws at me, even if it's just to put him in his place before telling him we're done "playing" with magic together. "Okay," I sigh, pretending to be bored. "How?"

He laughs again, a low, slightly dirty noise over the phone. "One word. Bowling."

Memory Lanes is firmly stuck in 1954, all atomic-age chic and pistachio-green Formica, and way on the other side of town. Bay picks me up at the 7-Eleven around the corner from the movie theater, and I decide not to focus on how slimy and backdoor it seems as we pull up later in the afternoon.

"Hope you brought your bowling shoes," he says, grinning as I get in.

"Whose car is this?" He's driving a sugary silver Audi that looks brand-new.

"Fiona's stepmom's," he says as he pulls away from the curb. His coat is open, and a soft gray scarf is looped loosely around his neck. "She's in Hawaii or somewhere else tropical and decadent."

I blink. "With Fiona's dad? And where is Fiona anyway?"

"Unclear. On the first part." He takes a corner at a speed that definitely seems unsafe if not illegal, and I grab the dashboard. "Fiona is sleeping off a little too much frivolity."

"But she doesn't mind you taking her stepmom's car?"

"So many questions!" He smiles broadly and pats my knee. "Relax, little bird. We're not running away to Mexico, we're just going bowling."

I hate the heat in my cheeks. "I hope you're not expecting me to be good."

"You can be as good as you want to be, you know," he says, and turns to look at me, brow furrowed in amusement. "No stopping you."

It hadn't even occurred to me, actually. But I'm so used to hiding what I can do, sometimes at home I forget I can use a little boost here and there. I painted my nails the other night, and ruined one ten minutes later. Instead of closing my eyes and focusing, I took it all off with nail polish remover, and it wasn't until I was in bed that I realized how dumb that was.

But that's my problem, and it doesn't have anything to do with him, or why I'm here.

Bay throws an arm over my shoulder when we walk in, steering me toward the far left-hand lane. It's a strange weight, and for a minute all I can smell beyond the stale sweat of old shoes and industrial carpet is his coat, warm wool that's somehow spicy, like a far-off land. My nose tickles, and I duck out from under it by pretending to sneeze.

Suddenly I'm really glad we're heading toward a group of people, since Fiona isn't around.

"Afternoon, bowlers," Bay says, shrugging off his coat and tossing it casually over the back of the booth at the head of the lane. "This is Wren."

"Prepare to be amazed by my skills, Wren," a boy in a Dr. Who T-shirt tells me. His hair is nearly shoulder length, too brown to be blond and too blond to be brown, and his nose ring is a shiny silver loop with a ball balanced in the center. He ambles up to the lane and sort of jerks into motion; the ball lurches forward, spinning crazily, and knocks down six pins.

"Formidable," I say politely, and a girl in a short red dress and a long white sweater laughs. She doesn't look familiar, either, and I wonder if these are all Summerhill kids.

"I'm Leah," she says, "and that's Tommy, since Bay has forgotten his manners. And over there are Antonia and Clay." She points at a boy and a girl coming back from the snack bar with one giant fountain soda and an order of cheese fries on wax paper in a pink plastic basket.

Jude isn't here, but I can hear her voice in my head: *"Just be careful."*

I shake it off and drop my coat on top of Bay's before sitting down. "I need shoes."

"No problem." Leah leans over and drags my feet into her lap. "Nice Docs. Hold on." She pulls a black velvet pouch out of her pocket and from it a small mirror. Its surface is cloudy, smeared with something, and she holds it in front of my feet as she says softly, "Magick mirror in my hand, see my need, heed my plan. Show the shoes Wren must wear, hide these boots from every stare. In this glass your power I see, my intent, my will, so mote it be."

The air shimmers with an audible sigh, and the scuffed black leather on my feet melts away to reveal faded blue-and-white bowling shoes. Leah bows her head with a quick smile, and I pull my feet off her lap.

"Very nice," I tell her, honest this time, and twist my feet in different directions. I can still feel the worn-in leather of my boots around my ankles, the familiar weight of them, but I can only see the shoes.

Bay golf-claps with a smirk that somehow doesn't seem as pleased as it should be, and I get up to look for a ball.

"Who's the new girl?" Antonia asks as she sits down at the next table, jerking her head in my direction. Leah has gotten up to bowl, and Tommy takes her place in the chair. I glance over my shoulder to see him looking at Bay, as if he needs permission before he speaks, so I call, "I'm Wren. Hi."

Antonia just stares and takes a noisy slurp of the soda before Clay snatches it away. "Be nice, loser. Hey, Wren. Ignore the resident bitch."

Antonia rolls her eyes, bright blue ones lined in an even more obnoxious blue, and ignores me as she reaches for a fry dripping with orange cheese.

"No fighting, boys and girls," Bay says lightly, but he's staring at the fries intently. When Antonia picks up another one, it's dripping with what looks like toxic waste, and smells like it even from where I'm standing.

"Jesus, Bay." She throws it down and grabs a napkin, wiping her hands furiously. "I fucking paid for those."

He lifts his brows innocently and snaps his fingers, and the cheese is back. Antonia snorts. "Like I'd eat it now."

"She's on the rag," Clay mock-whispers behind one hand, looking at me.

"Oh my God." She practically pushes him out of the booth so she can stomp away to the bathroom. In her skinny jeans and prom-pink sweater, her blond hair swinging against her back, she looks like Barbie's evil twin.

Bay gets up to join me, casually looping his arm over my shoulders again. "Antonia there isn't like us. She's a ghost chaser, likes to play séance every once in a while. I'm pretty sure she's convinced she's a reincarnated spirit, and Clay hasn't tried to tell her otherwise. He's psychic, so he'd know, I guess."

I glance at Clay, by-the-book All-American in his rugby shirt and jeans, dark brush cut and freckles. "And he . . . likes her?"

Bay smirks. "There's no explaining true love."

Tommy is in love with Leah, he tells me, and since Tommy is generally extremely stoned, he doesn't really notice the magic going on around him. He learned not to question it, either, apparently, which sounds sort of ominous to me. Leah isn't a natural, but she uses spell craft really well—one of those determined straight-A students, I bet, who aces calculus and physics even when she's really a lit geek who's better at writing drippy poetry.

It's a weird soup, but Bay connects some more of the dots—Leah is a Saint Francis grad, which is how she knows Fiona and therefore Bay; Tommy is a tagalong. Antonia is a Summerhill student who had a crush on Bay, and one he milked for a while before he realized she was made of equal parts boobs and poison. Clay met Antonia at a party a few months ago, and either knows she's a decent person deep down, or enjoys the naked parts of her too much to care.

"More than I needed to know," I tell him, making a face.

Leah jumps up when a tiny Asian girl walks in, and waves her toward our lanes. "Alison's here!"

"Now she's a natural," Bay says under his breath. "But she's not sure what to do with it. Big-time repression."

His running commentary is getting on my nerves, as well as his hovering. He's always a little too close, a little too friendly, and trying to convince myself that he wasn't jealous when I brought Gabriel to the party the other night isn't working too well anymore.

Sometimes I hate boys.

Antonia reappears just after Leah introduces me to Alison, who's so shy, she barely looks at me. It doesn't matter. I'm determined to get through this.

And for a little while, I manage to at least ignore Antonia. Tommy is pretty amusing, even if he is herbally enhanced, and Leah is great. It isn't until Clay gets up to help Alison improve her aim that Antonia lets her snark off the leash again.

"Aren't you supposed to be able to do that on your own?" she calls, casually waving a chewed-on straw in Alison's direction. "Put on some grown-up panties, sweetie."

Alison blanches, hair hanging in her face, and Clay straightens up with a frown.

"Tonia, seriously. Turn it down a notch or seventeen."

She snorts, rolling her eyes again. "Oh, come on. If she could turn me into a toad, or do anything halfway impressive, I'd like to see it. The girl can barely tie her own shoes."

That's it. A single tear is rolling down Alison's cheek, and I don't bother to think twice. I turn to Antonia and focus hard, power funneling up out of me in a single, precise blast.

Antonia chokes, coughs, grabs at her throat, and a moment later spits a tiny, gnarled toad off her tongue.

Even Clay snickers.

Antonia is snarling, and Tommy is busy chasing the toad when Bay drags me away, and I let him. He marches me past the snack bar and the rental desk, and down a short hall that leads to the bathroom.

"I think you just made a mortal enemy, sweetheart," he laughs, and hugs me before I can protest.

"Don't call me that." I'm shaking with rage and the last trembling vibration of energy, and I'm not proud of myself.

Even if Antonia totally deserves worse.

"God, that was awesome." He's not even looking at me, but he's grinning like a satisfied cat. "Quick thinking, thematically appropriate. Very hot."

I blink and realize he's turned to face me again, one

hand reaching out to stroke my cheek. Gently, fondly, and I'm so busy panicking, it takes me a minute to get my hands between us and shove at his chest.

Not before he kisses me, though, and I want to spit. It's cool, too wet, and so wrong, I'm stunned.

"Oh my God, what is your deal?" I shove harder when he doesn't step right back. "I thought you were with Fiona!"

He shrugs, wiping his mouth with the back of one hand casually. "I am, more or less."

"More or less? What does that mean?" I splutter.

"It means she amuses me, and she likes to get her freak on, and she spends her daddy's money on me like it's water," he explains, and every trace of the friendly, slightly smarmy guy I know is gone.

His eyes are as cold and dead as Danny's ever were.

"Oh my God, you are such scum." I shake my head, and push him, hard. "I had no idea."

"Oh, come on, Wren," he says, grabbing my arm. For a moment, he tries on something that I think is supposed to look like pleading innocence, but it slips when I make a retching noise. "She can't even do spell work. I do everything for her, just to make her happy and shut her up. She mumbles something in pigeon Latin, and I make it happen for her. But you. You're the real deal, Wren.

You have power like I've never seen, and unless I'm way off the mark, you haven't even tried to spread your little magical wings. You have no idea what we could do together."

"And you have no idea how very wrong you are," I hiss, and this time I push with the power inside me. He staggers back against the wall, and I hold him there as I back away. "Whatever this was, it's over."

I run back to the lanes and grab my coat. Antonia and Clay are over by the jukebox, and Leah has one arm around Alison. Tommy pops up from beneath one of the tables with the toad in his hand, and chuckles. "Adam would have loved that. Dude, it's so frigging tiny."

I freeze at the name *Adam*, even with Bay striding toward me, his face sculpted into a mask of fury. It all makes sense now—Fiona going to Saint Francis, the violence Gabriel sensed in Bay, Jude's warning to be careful.

For one horrible moment, I think I'm actually going to puke, right here in the middle of Memory Lanes.

But Bay is still coming at me, and Leah is saying, "Where did he transfer to again? We never hear from him anymore," and I need to be not here, right now.

"Don't even think about it," I say to Bay, ignoring the others. I have one hand up, as if I'm going to hold him off with that. But he knows better and stops a good ten feet away.

"Wren?" Leah says, but I don't answer.

And then I'm running, past Bay, past the desk, out the door, and away from all the brand-new mistakes I've made.

# CHAPTER TWENTY

I'M HALFWAY HOME WHEN I CAN'T TAKE IT anymore. Sometime during the afternoon it started to snow, and I'm not dressed for such a long walk. My scarf and boots are soaked, and the only gloves I have are my fingerless ones. I duck under the shelter of a gas station and get out my phone to call home for a ride.

There's a text from Darcia, short and sweet: TALKED 2 T. AGAIN!!! I'm so distracted it takes me a minute to realize she must mean Thierry. Which is cool, but something to deal with later.

When I dial the house, no one answers. That's strange, since it's Sunday and I know Mom is home. I try her cell, and it goes to voice mail. Perfect.

I'm shivering, lips and fingertips numb, even though the cold hasn't iced over my fury at Bay. That's still burning, a low, steady flame. I just wish it would actually keep me warm.

It's already getting dark, and in the soft fog of snow, it's hard to see. I pull out my phone one last time and try Mari, who picks up on the first ring.

"Wren?"

"Hey." I clench my jaw to keep my teeth from chattering. "Could you possibly give me a ride?"

"I was just on my way to your house, actually." She sounds distracted. "Where are you?"

I tell her, and when she pulls up ten minutes later I'm bouncing from foot to foot and rubbing my hands together. "Thank you so much," I say as I climb into the car, holding my hands out to the heating vents once the door is closed. "I don't know where Mom is, but I was all the way over at Memory Lanes."

Mari pulls back onto Mountain Avenue, the tires skidding in the first slushy coat of snow. "She's home, with Robin. That's why I was heading over there."

I'm not following, and I'm still too cold to concentrate. "What do you mean?"

Mari frowns, and pushes the car into the next gear. All I can do is hold on.

★ ★ ★

I can feel the magic as soon as Mari and I walk in. The air is trembling, echoes of power still shimmering and settling. It smells like ozone and burnt sugar, and there's no question whatever happened is Not Good.

"Rose?" Mari unwinds her scarf slowly, glancing into the kitchen and then up the stairs.

I peel off all of my wet things and my boots, leaving them in a heap by the door. There's movement upstairs, and I take the steps two at a time.

Mom is just coming out of Robin's room, and she looks like the victim of a battle. Her hair is coming out of its clip in a million crazy directions, there's a smudge of soot on one cheek, and a book in her hands.

One of my books. The one no one is supposed to know about.

"Downstairs, now." Her voice is a shredded husk, and I swallow hard.

Mari is standing in the middle of the kitchen when I follow Mom into the room. Her mouth is hanging open, and mine follows. Smoke has left burnt trails on the wall, and the table is pushed up against the pantry door. One chair lies on its side, and the seat is splintered. Melted candle wax is stuck in hard, white clumps all over the table and the floor beside it, and the kitchen counter is a mess of herbs and spices and other things I can't identify.

Our biggest pot is still on the stove, a bubbled crust dripping over its lip.

Holy crap.

"What happened?" Mari asks before I can. She steps over a broken dish and a pile of feathers and rights the chair.

"I left Robin here so I could go to the grocery store and run a few other quick errands, and I came home to this." Mom sets the book down on one of the table's few clear spots and leans against the counter. "And what I think was a ghost, as well as a hysterical twelve-year-old."

"Oh my God." The words are barely audible around the hand Mari's holding to her mouth, but the tone is pretty clear.

Meanwhile, I'm still stuck on *ghost*. "What was she trying to do?"

"Summon your father, apparently," Mom says, turning hard brown eyes on me. She points at the table. "With a spell she had no idea how to use, not that it was the right one anyway. What I want to know is what the hell you were doing with a book like that? Robin told me she found it in your room."

I can't lie my way out of this one. I mean, I *could*, but I can't. Not anymore.

Even if I don't plan to admit exactly why I needed those books.

"I was, um, curious." The laser glare of Mom's gaze pulls my spine straighter. "I just wanted to see what magic was all about, you know? All kinds of magic."

"Sam?" Mari is saying, shaking her head. She's still stunned, all of the color drained from her face. "Sam is . . . not dead. You can't summon a living person! I mean . . . can you?"

"If you can, that's a kind of magic I want absolutely nothing to do with." Mom scrubs a hand over her face, and her exhaustion is right there in the way her hand shakes, the faint shuddering breath she draws.

*Summon your father.* I still can't believe it. I want to strangle Robin and hug her and scream at her all at the same time.

"There was a . . . ghost?" I manage to ask, trying to picture it. "Whose ghost?"

"I have no idea," Mom says, and she actually laughs a little. "I'm not even sure where I sent it. I haven't done magic like that off the top of my head in a long time. Maybe never."

Mari stands up and pushes the table aside to get into the pantry for the broom. "And Robin?"

"Is asleep." Mom sighs and pushes off the counter to

help. "She's grounded into her next three lives, but she's okay. She didn't hurt herself anyway, and she didn't burn the house down."

"Well, that's good." I shake off the fog of shock and get the pot from the stove, intending to take it to the sink to soak it. I'm holding it, and the nasty stench coming from it, away from my body when Mom says, "Wren? There's something you should know."

I can't think of what else there could be on top of what I learned about Bay and Adam, and the fact that my baby sister apparently lost her mind this afternoon. I set the pot in the sink and turn around. "Yeah?"

"I called your dad. He's coming to see you both."

Gabriel is heading toward me when I round the corner twenty minutes later, and I don't even pretend to have pride. I run straight into his arms. I have no idea how he happened to be right there, but I don't care. Maybe he could sense the ginormous freak-out brewing in my head.

"Hey, whoa, what happened?" he says after a minute, pulling back to look me in the eye. "You didn't answer your phone, and I was coming to talk to you."

My only answer is a muffled sob, and he holds me tighter. "Just tell me . . . are you okay?"

I finally step back, wiping the hot tears off my cheek with the back of one hand. "I don't know. Can we go somewhere?"

He smiles and smoothes my hair out of my eyes. "Always."

"Better?"

I'm wrapped up in a blanket on the sofa, with a pair of Gabriel's thick socks on my feet and a hot mug of tea. I nod, trying not to sniffle. "A little."

"Okay, so." He sits down and puts his arm around the giant lump of me inside the blanket. "What happened?"

I take a deep breath and set the tea down on the coffee table. "Robin tried to . . . *summon* our dad. Which, you know, would be like teleportation if it even worked, and that's just insane, so what she got was a hot mess all over the kitchen and apparently a ghost, which my mom had to . . . I don't know, banish or something, she's not even sure, but after that, I guess because Robin is having some kind of dramatic preteen meltdown about it, she called him, our dad, and he's coming. Here. To see us."

Gabriel blinks and opens his mouth. He shuts it again, and then looks up at me. "Um. Wow."

"Yeah."

It's too much, all at once. Everything I believed about

Bay, and even Fiona, was just an illusion, some pink, pretty lie I told myself to get away with using magic when and where I wanted to. And I can't help wondering if my memories of my dad are nothing more than that— an illusion, a half-remembered fairy tale I embellished with a strong, handsome father and a happy little girl.

If one more thing shatters, it's going to be my heart.

I'm shocked to see that, now that the surprise has sunk in, Gabriel looks relieved.

"Um, I'm having, like, major trauma here," I say, curling deeper into the blanket.

"I know, I'm sorry." He hugs me tighter, kisses the top of my head. "But maybe it won't be so bad. I mean, you were going to face this eventually, right? So now you'll, you know, get it over with." His gaze is far away, and he still looks strangely pleased. Like this is the answer to all of my problems or something, which I really doubt.

"I'm just not ready for this. Not with . . ." Now I'm the one who's not telling all, and at this rate we could probably talk around each other all night.

"With what?"

I smile weakly. "Just . . . everything. It's been a weird couple of weeks, you know?"

He bites his bottom lip, gray eyes searching my face. "Trust me, this will be good. I mean, it'll help. It'll . . .

really. Believe me."

Suspicion curls like smoke in my stomach. "How can you possibly know that? How can you—" And then it hits me. I'm so stupid, so very, very stupid. "You *do* know. You know something about this, about my dad. Don't you?" When he looks away, I fight my way out of the quilt and grab his arm. "Don't you?"

He starts to shake his head, and I glare at him. "Don't even lie. Not now. Just *tell* me."

He lays his head on the back of the sofa to stare at the ceiling. "I didn't mean to. I swear, Wren, I didn't mean to. But at Christmas, when your mom started talking about my dad, I was . . . I was just so pissed off, and I wasn't trying hard enough to control it, and I . . ." He takes a shaky breath, and I dig my fingers into his arm.

"Gabriel, come *on*. What is it?"

"I just had this flash from her, and it was all this stuff about your dad." He picks his head up and looks at me, and I shiver. The relief is gone.

"What about him?"

"It's more impressions and feelings, remember, but . . ." He takes a deep breath this time, but he doesn't look away. He doesn't chicken out. "He has powers, too, Wren. And he can't use them anymore. He . . . it's like he poisoned himself with them or something."

Even when Ryan called to tell me Danny had died, I didn't feel this dizzy. I'm sitting, but the room seems to spin away from me anyway, and I squeeze my eyes shut.

It makes all the sense in the world. It's why I'm more powerful than Mom and Aunt Mari, and why Robin is, too. I can't believe I never even considered it.

Now I understand why Gabriel has been so worried about me doing magic, and I think of all the things I've been doing with Bay, the things Robin did today. I can hear Gabriel's voice in my head: *Poisoned himself* . . .

"Oh God." I push away the blanket, kicking my feet free, and Gabriel grabs my arm.

"Wait, Wren, just think about it for a minute. I don't know everything, I only get impressions unless I'm trying, you know that."

I wrench my arm free and stumble to my feet, fighting to see the room in focus. It swims in shifting shadows instead, and I lurch away from the couch. All these years, and Mom never said anything. Never even hinted. If anything is a betrayal, that's the worst.

"Wren, let's talk, okay? I mean, maybe it's not that bad, but at least you'll know. Wren?"

I can hear him following me, but I can't answer. I'm crying too hard.

# CHAPTER TWENTY-ONE

"ARE YOU SURE THAT'S ENOUGH FOR LUNCH, sweetie?" Mrs. Lattimer says the next morning. She's hovering, mostly dressed for work minus her shoes and lipstick, and her briefcase and keys and coffee are piled on one end of the counter. "I can give you some money if you want to get a sandwich, too. You girls eat like birds. I don't even know how you get through the day."

"This is fine, thanks." I smile at her, or try to, and shake my paper bag of yogurt, fruit, and peanut butter crackers. It's what I take all the time, and the thought of food still doesn't sit well anyway.

Gabriel was the one to go to my house and pack a bag for me after I called my mom and told her there was no way I was coming home. She didn't argue, and I was so wiped out, I couldn't process how surprising that was, even though I told her I was angriest at her for keeping the truth about my father's magic from me.

Mom wouldn't let me stay at Gabriel's, which I mostly expected, but Jess's parents were glad to have me for a few days. I have no idea what my mother said to Mrs. Lattimer on the phone, but they've been treating me the way I guess most people would treat an unidentified explosive.

I don't mind, really. I don't feel like talking, to anyone. Even Jess didn't try, although she curled up behind me in her big bed last night and stroked my hair until I finally went to sleep.

Mrs. Lattimer drives us to school, which is a bonus since it snowed hard enough to leave a few inches, and the day is crystal cold, brittle with ice. Gabriel's waiting at my locker, and I don't even care who's watching—I kiss him hard, pretending just for a minute that I can swallow some of his calm steadiness.

Once I'd cried myself out, I told him about Adam. I wanted everything spread out in one place so I could try to make them neat and orderly facts instead of a throbbing panicked pulse in my head, and that meant telling him what I'd learned about Bay, and what I'd been doing.

Part of me was cringing, waiting for him to say it was too messed up, too much, but he didn't. I'll always be grateful for that. Not to mention the chance to do something about a missing kid and take my mind off how furious I am at my mother.

Gabriel and I walk to homeroom together. Dar passes us in the hallway, holding Thierry's hand, her cheeks pink as an Easter egg, and I give her a subtle thumbs-up. Then I give Gabriel a kiss on the cheek, just because.

Once Gabriel and I are at our desks, I lean over. "Any ideas?"

"About . . . you know?" He shakes his head. Without confronting Bay, which doesn't seem really likely to end happily, we've been trying to figure out some way to learn more about him. I can just picture interrogating Audrey, and drowning in a flood of tears and outrage. Without her, though, I'm stuck.

Unless . . .

"Hey, is Olivia working today?"

He shakes his head again, frowning. "She usually has Monday off. Why?"

I grin at him, possibilities racing through my head. "How do you think she would feel about taking you on a prospective student tour of Saint Francis?"

★ ★ ★

"There's no way they're going to believe I could afford this school," Olivia says as we chug across town in the VW. "Especially not if they see us drive up in this thing."

Gabriel laughs. "I doubt they're going to be watching out the window."

"Shut up, you," Olivia grumbles, fingering the stiff, white collar of her shirt. "I'm not an actress, you know. What if they ask questions? What if they want to talk about the application process first? What if—"

"Dude," Gabriel says, glancing at her from the passenger seat. "Relax. We can always just walk out."

"Dude?" Olivia says, but she's trying not to smile. I snicker in the backseat.

My smile fades a minute later when my phone buzzes again. It's the fifth text in an hour, and I know exactly who it is without even looking. My stomach turns as I reach into my pocket to look anyway.

U CANT KEEP THIS UP 4EVR. U KNOW HOW MUCH FUN WE HAD.

Bay. I delete it and tuck my phone away, nauseated. How he can believe I'm going to forgive him after yesterday is beyond me, but Gabriel thinks he's worried because he knows I heard Adam's name.

"That's probably true," I said when he proposed his theory, and he shrugged. I haven't told him how often

Bay has texted since the first two, though, because Gabriel may be understanding, but he's not a saint.

And he's convinced that something awful happened to Adam at Bay's hands. "I *felt* blood, Wren," he explained, "and no one has seen Adam in weeks. Put it together."

I don't want to, really. I can't imagine a kid my age murdered, especially not by other kids. It's too huge to consider, wrong on levels that I can't even comprehend.

But going to Saint Francis is one possible way to figure out something helpful. As we pull into the parking lot, I cross my fingers.

A woman is waiting for us in the office. I'm not sure if I was expecting a nun, but this chick looks like any other corporate worker bee in her navy suit and red scarf. She eyes me with curiosity, and I try to make myself as small and unobtrusive as possible. Gabriel holds my hand anyway.

"I have some information to gather for you," she says after shaking hands with Olivia and introducing herself as Valerie Flynn. "Why don't you take a look around while I do, get a sense of the school?"

It's hard not to beam. Letting us wander around on our own is the best-case scenario, and I'm betting that Adam's locker is going to have the equivalent of a neon sign above it. When Danny died, there were stickers and notes all over his locker within days, and flowers stuck through the vent in the door.

Students are still milling around, coming out of the band room and the hallway that leads to the auditorium, where someone is practicing a song that sounds like something from a musical. A couple of kids break out of a lip-lock against the lockers at the end of the upstairs hall when they hear us coming, and another girl walks past us into the bathroom, door squealing shut behind her.

"I don't see anything," Olivia whispers as we walk along, poking our heads into classrooms just to keep up the act. "Maybe they wouldn't let the kids decorate his locker?"

"No, they did," Gabriel says, and points as we round a corner. Halfway down the hall, one locker is covered in Post-it Notes and stickers. Dying flowers are stuck in the vents, and three teddy bears and a floppy-eared stuffed dog sit on the floor in front of it.

Olivia and I stand back, watching the hall for anyone coming, while Gabriel goes straight for the dial on the locker. It's the one thing Adam would have touched every day, I guess, and I realize I'm holding my breath as Gabriel curls his fingers around it and closes his eyes.

"I'm not sold on this as worth the money," Olivia whispers to me. She's looking at a bulletin board announcing events. "Of course, who knows? Maybe they have some kind of Skull and Bones club that gets graduates into Congress or something."

"I think they'd have to drape themselves in ivy first," I say absently, watching Gabriel. He's concentrating so hard, brows drawn together and mouth pinched shut, and then all of a sudden he's not.

Because his knees are buckling, and he's crumpled on the floor before I can even blink.

"Shit," I hiss, and smack Olivia on the arm.

He's gasping for breath, and I know it's another headache. Olivia is horrified, hovering beside me in her gray pencil skirt and clutching his hand.

"Wren, what the hell? Is he okay?"

"He will be." *I hope.* But I don't know how we're going to get him downstairs and into the car like this, not without someone freaking out and calling 911. He's shaking violently this time.

Unless I hide him. I frown, thinking hard. "Go back downstairs and tell that woman we had to leave—tell her I was sick or something. I'll get him down to the car."

She lets go of her brother's hand reluctantly. "How?"

"I'm working on it," I tell her. "Just go."

The hallway is empty except for me and Gabriel, and I lean close. His breathing has evened out, and I stroke his cheek. "Hey. Can you hear me? Gabriel?"

He manages to crack one eye open. "Adam." He sounds like he has a throat full of glass.

"Tell me later," I say, and wedge an arm under his shoulders. "You need to help a little. Gabriel, come on, you can do it."

His head lolls on his shoulders like one of those stupid bobblehead dolls, and I give up and *push* at him with my power. For a moment he's weightless, and then finally he balances, blinking.

"Now hold still," I tell him. My heart's pounding, because I have no idea if this will work, and I can hear Gabriel's voice in the back of my head: *Poisoned himself with power.* But if Bay could do this with Fiona, I can, too. I tug him as close as possible while he winces, and wave my hand in front of both of us as I whisper, "Invisible."

Something like static crackles under my skin for a second, but when I look down, I can still see us both. Crap. Then a short boy in a loosened tie and his blazer hanging over one shoulder skids around the corner, laughing. I have to shove Gabriel closer to the lockers so he won't run over us.

It worked. I can't quite believe it, but it worked.

Steering Gabriel all the way downstairs and out to the car isn't easy, though. More than once I have to shush him when he mutters something random: "the stupid French Revolution" and "tell her no way" and "Tater Tots." We're invisible, but I'm pretty sure anyone could hear us talking.

He's a lot heavier than he looks, and I nearly crack his head on the car door trying to wrestle him inside. I sit with him in the back, focusing very hard on not remembering Danny beside me in this same backseat, blank and trusting and doomed. Gabriel finally lays his head on my shoulder, and I murmur comforting nonsense things I won't remember a moment later into his hair.

Olivia startles me when she opens the door, and once inside she draws a shuddering breath and says, "Shit, where are they?"

Oh. Crap. I whisper, "We're back here, hold on," so I don't scare the shit out of her, and pull my power into a neat knot as I say, "Um, visible."

I wriggle against the same tingling crackle under my skin, and smile at Olivia in the rearview mirror.

"Wow," she says, blinking. "Is he okay?"

"Let's just get out of here," I tell her, and she starts the engine without another word.

"I saw him," Gabriel says when we're two blocks away, and lifts his head to face me. At least he sounds lucid, even though he looks deflated, pale and fragile, circles smudged under his eyes in purple. "He was just a kid. But it was so much . . ."

"I know." I grab his hand and squeeze it, holding on, and jerk when my phone buzzes in my jacket pocket.

I know who it is without even looking. I reach into my pocket to shut it off, and let Olivia take us home.

# CHAPTER TWENTY-TWO

IT'S A LONG, STRANGE WEEK. PARTS OF ME ARE scattered all over town—at Jess's in the evening, with Gabriel at school, at Bliss for two shifts. The part of me that wonders what's happening at home is a raw wound, too sore to touch, and the part of me waiting for my father to get into town is cringing in a corner, too frightened to even peek out.

Gabriel is a rock, even though his last headache won't completely fade. He's dreaming, too, he tells me on Thursday morning.

"I don't know what might be real and what's just the images I saw at Adam's locker, trying to shape themselves into some kind of sense." He pokes at his sandwich at lunch, as if he expects it to move or poke him back. "Then there are the dreams where I'm running Bay out of town at the end of a flamethrower, but I think that's just wishful thinking."

"Aw." I pat his hand and lean up to kiss him lightly. Gabriel may have vengeance in his heart, but he's the gentlest person I've ever met. He'd probably wind up saying please as he brandished his flamethrower.

I can take care of Bay on my own anyway, which I'm sure he knows. It's Adam that's a big empty space, and I have no idea what to do about it. When I close my eyes, I picture the kid I remember, not too tall, dark brown hair always cut a little too short, lying somewhere in a sticky puddle of drying blood.

His eyes are open and unseeing.

I shudder and unwrap the granola bar Mrs. Lattimer tucked in my hand this morning. I'm not really hungry, but there's nothing else to do while Gabriel faces down his sandwich, and Jess is across the room with Cal. Sitting in his lap, actually, which is something I never thought I would witness in my lifetime. Unless I'm wrong, she's batting her eyelashes at him.

At least someone's happy. Dar will be, too, on Saturday morning, but until she gets through the showcase on

Friday night, she's going to be the walking bundle of raw nerves she's been for days. I keep finding her practicing her fingering under her desk during World Lit. If you don't know what she's doing, it looks sort of disturbing.

Kirk Burdett was staring at her yesterday, snickering and pointing her out to another one of his knuckle-dragging buddies. I was so tempted to send an electric shock across the desks, possibly to his crotch. But at the last moment I just glared. I haven't used my power at all since Monday at Saint Francis.

Maybe it's dumb. It's not like magic would be out of character for me, even at school. And when Mom and I had it out a few months ago, she didn't say it was dangerous. But what does she know? She's not the one who apparently abused it, and she clearly didn't think enough about it to even tell us our dad had magic in his blood, too.

It's another empty place inside me, made purely out of confusion, but if I get close enough I can feel my power underneath it, a vague, humming vibration. For now, I can't bring myself to touch it.

"You're not eating."

I glance up at Gabriel and roll my eyes. "Neither are you."

"We can starve together," he says with a dry smile. "It

will be beautiful and tragic, and people will write songs about us."

"With my luck, Katy Perry will write the song, and we'll die in glow-in-the-dark tracksuits," I grumble, and he snorts a laugh.

My phone vibrates in my pocket, and I groan. Bay has stopped texting so often, but not entirely.

Gabriel frowns and pokes me. "See who it is, Wren. It can't always be him."

And he's right. It's my mom, with an entirely too grammatically correct text telling me my dad is finally here.

I show it to Gabriel without a word. Tonight, I'm going home.

There's an unfamiliar car parked outside the house, a faded gray sedan that nearly disappears in the dusk. I run my hand over the hood, but I'm not Gabriel—it simply feels like cold metal. I don't know how much of my father would linger in the hood of his car anyway.

I can't stall anymore. I have my packed bag in one hand and my backpack over one shoulder, and I'm going numb as I stand staring at the house. In the thick gray shadows, the windows glow softly, and I can see someone moving behind the sheer curtains. This is it.

The door opens before I'm even halfway up the walk, and Robin slouches there, toes wriggling in her striped socks and her hair loose around her face. So she can hide behind it, I think, and raise my free hand in a sort of half-mast wave.

"I missed you," she says once I'm close enough to hear her.

"You too. Are you okay?" I glance at the windows one last time before she moves aside to let me in.

"Yeah." She shrugs, but she's strung pretty taut, and the hands she has jammed in her jeans pockets are curled into fists.

I bump her shoulder and work my mouth into a smile. "Let's do this then."

She closes the door while I drop my bags at the foot of the stairs and take off my coat. I'm a little amazed at how scared I am. I can't remember a time when I haven't spoken to my mom for this long, but right now I'm tempted to run into the living room and hide myself in her arms.

And my dad . . .

I turn around with Robin plastered against my right side, and there he is. I wonder if I'm still breathing—I feel too light, unreal, made of nothing but memory. He's the man I knew, beneath a new layer of years that licked gray through his hair and his beard. And yet, I don't know him at all.

"Hello, Wren."

His voice is familiar, even if the smile hiding in his whiskers is a little dim. The one I loved was huge, mouth open and teeth white, always full of laughter.

All of my words are tangled in my throat, wrapped in fear and rage and grief and a strange, hopeful joy. I can't remember the last time we were all in one room, and I don't know if my mom realizes it, but suddenly she's striding toward me.

"I missed you, baby," she whispers, and then she's all around me, scent and warmth and softness. "Let's do this, huh?"

I have to laugh, because it's so close to what I said to Robin, but a tear escapes anyway. As Mom wipes it away, I whisper, "I'm still mad at you, you know."

She kisses the top of my head. "I figured. Now come on."

The dining room table feels weirdly like a council of war. My parents take one side, and Robin and I take the other, and the two ends float uselessly, empty.

Robin can't shut up. She's a little machine gun of questions, punching holes in the mystery of our dad. It's not that I don't want to know that he used to be an art teacher and now he illustrates children's books and fantasy novels, or that he lives up in the Adirondacks, where he spends a lot of time reading and hiking. But it's hard to listen when all I can see is my mom, watching him answer as if every word is a gift, and my dad, glancing sidelong at my mom every few minutes, like he needs to know she's still there, real, in the same room.

They look like the kind of long-lost lovers you see in movies, and the ache of it is palpable in the way they don't touch.

And Robin doesn't have any idea how much more she doesn't know, and doesn't even know to ask.

I'm studying my dad's face—the spiderweb of lines I don't remember beside his eyes, the eyes themselves that are so much browner than in my memories, the hands that look smaller now that I'm bigger. Sometimes he catches me watching, and I'm surprised that he never looks away.

Well, if I'm allowed to see him now, I want to see everything.

Robin's asking what his house is like, if he has extra bedrooms, and I get it, she wants an invitation, she wants to see it all herself, too, but as he smiles at her, I can't wait anymore. "Robin, just . . . shut up for a minute."

She huffs and reaches out to smack my arm, but I

grab her hand, stopping it in midair, and stare right at my father. Dad. Sam Darby. I don't even know what to call him anymore.

"Tell me why you left, really. And why Mom never told us you have power, too."

Robin gasps, and I let go of her hand as she swivels around to face him. Mom isn't shocked, of course. She is pale, though, facing Robin across the table like she's waiting for a blow.

"It's not a short story," Dad says. He's worrying the wedding band, which he still wears, with his thumb, twisting it. "And it's not a very happy one."

"I want to know," I say, and I'm proud that my voice is steady.

Beside me, Robin straightens up. "Yeah. Me too."

"Okay then." He stands up and walks toward the window, looking out at the darkness, and the whole room seems to go still, even the air unmoving as we wait for him to speak. When he turns around again, he looks hollowed out, and every secret he has to tell is there in his eyes.

An hour later, Robin is curled beside Mom on the sofa, and I'm cross-legged in front of the fire, the heat licking at my back. My father is in the chair in the corner, elbows on his knees, head bent, and I can't decide whether I want to hit him or hug him.

It's like Gabriel said, more or less. His family had power, both boys and girls, but it wasn't as persistent as I guess my mom's family's has been. Not everyone had power, and not everyone could use it well. According to Dad, it was treated more like an inherited disease than a gift.

But he loved it. And he was good at it, almost from the beginning. Developing and practicing his magic was his one rebellion, and the only time he was any kind of happy, except when he was drawing.

He was a freshman in college when it got weird. Using his power was such a habit—getting a sandwich, turning on the TV, typing a paper—that the magic, as he said, started using him.

"I didn't even think about it half the time." His voice is tired, rueful. "It was a little like, um, impulse shopping, I guess you call it. Before I even knew I wanted something, or was angry about something, or needed something, the power was working. I got so used to that constant buzz, I realized I couldn't remember what it felt like not to use my power. And that scared the shit out of me."

Robin had blinked at that and blushed a little, but

Dad had kept talking as if he didn't even realize what he'd said.

And I thought about the picture my power had taken, all on its own, of my friends at the café.

Dad had stopped himself then, even though he didn't explain exactly how. It had involved borrowing a friend's apartment for a couple days, and I think possibly something to make him sleep, even though he didn't offer the details. At the end of a week, he hadn't used magic at all, and he decided that he wasn't going to use it ever again. It wasn't heroin, and it wasn't gambling, but he was an addict either way.

And then he met my mom.

I couldn't look at either of them when he said that.

"I never expected to meet someone who had power, too," he'd said, and the look he gave her was still full of wonder and shared secrets. They fell in love, the way people do, especially people attached by a thread the rest of the world doesn't even know exists. And he still didn't use his power, although he was happy to watch Mom and Aunt Mari, even my grandmother.

"But why . . . why did you leave then?" Robin says now, and Mom curls an arm around her shoulders.

I'm waiting to hear it in his own words, the whole story, not just the scrap of impression Gabriel had given me. No, that's not true. I'm waiting for something else, a different story, one with a better ending. I bite the inside of my lip, hard. This is anything but a fairy tale.

"It's my fault," Dad says carefully, looking at Robin and then at me. I can see now it's sadness that carved the lines beside his eyes. "My choices. I want you to understand that."

They were young, he says, without a lot of money. He was teaching, Mom was working at a salon, and all the things that you never expect to happen happened anyway. The car broke down, the salon closed, whatever it was that week. And he wanted to fix it.

So he was using magic again, just once in a while. And then I came along.

It's hard not to feel like it's my fault then, even though he keeps saying it's not.

We were babies, he says, babies who sometimes fell and hit their heads and swallowed too much mashed corn, and it happened all over again. Every instinct to keep us safe and happy bled out of him in magic, and he couldn't stop it. He wasn't even sure he wanted to try.

"You girls—all three of you"—he looks at Mom, and my heart squeezes painfully—"were everything to me. It didn't seem so dangerous then, if I could make sure no one had a concussion or there was always food on the table or even if I could make one of you laugh with dancing stuffed animals."

I'm not sure I understand. "Why was it so bad then?"

He takes a deep breath and squares his shoulders. Behind me, the fire crackles and spits. "It was like I felt a shadow behind me."

"Um, everyone has a shadow, Dad." The relief in Robin's voice is sweet-tart, as if she's just solved the stupidest problem ever, and wow, can't parents be dumb.

"Not that kind of a shadow," I tell her, and when Dad nods, my skin crawls, electric with dread.

"Not a real shadow, baby." He stands up and runs his hand softly over Robin's head before pacing the length of the room and back, his hands clenched as if he wants to grab something and choke the life out of it. He turns back to face us, and I flinch at the heartsick regret on his face. "I didn't know myself anymore. I couldn't trust myself. Things happened . . . bad things. When I was angry at someone at work, or stressed. I didn't have any control of it anymore. And I had no idea what I might do to you girls or your mother."

Robin snuggles a little closer to Mom, a tear sliding down one cheek, bright as a diamond.

"I stopped, of course. And it wasn't . . . pretty," he says, sitting down again. "But I can't use my power ever again. And I can't be around people who do use it, not for very long."

There's nothing left to say—he looks so tired, I know that he's told it all. Except one thing, I guess, and he says that now.

"I'm so sorry. Every day I'm sorry, every day I miss you. And I guess every day since the day I left, your mom and I have been screwing this up."

If he starts to cry, I'll be next, and I grit my teeth. If I cry now, I might never stop. The whole story is sad and stupid and careless and human and horrible. Like life can be, I guess.

But I don't know what any of it means when it comes to my story, *my* life. My power is nestled safe inside me, a vague, comfortable hum, but for the first time I'm really afraid of it.

"I know now that we should have told you everything." My mom's voice is low, rough. "When you were old enough for all of it, I mean. And . . . we didn't. I didn't. I was scared, too. But I think Robin was right." She squeezes Robin's shoulders. "Taking the problem right to the source is usually the smart thing."

For a second, the silence is too thick, too heavy, even with the fire snapping at the edges of it. And I think, *This is my family, the only one any of us have. And maybe it doesn't have to be a tragedy.*

So I smile at my dad, big and slow. "Maybe you can explain to her why summoning a living person is not ever the thing to do."

I'm lucky I don't singe my hair when Robin knocks me over with a sofa cushion, but I can hear my parents laughing. I like the sound of it.

# CHAPTER TWENTY-THREE

"THIS IS SUCH A BAD IDEA," GABRIEL WHISPERS as we sit down in the Book Barn the following night. It's packed, wooden folding chairs crammed into short rows around the stage, and the lights are already down. Jess and Cal are on the other side of Gabriel, holding hands and whispering something I'm pretty sure I should be glad I can't hear. I'm on the end, and there's barely two feet between me and the wall.

"We don't have another plan." I shrug, even though my heart is pounding. Gabriel can probably feel it even without his psychic senses. Inviting Bay and Fiona here is crazy. But when my mom said "taking the problem right to the source," I knew it was the only choice left. We certainly haven't been able to find out anything about Adam's disappearance on our own.

And I keep hearing Gabriel's voice in my head: *"Wren, there was blood."*

I shudder, and Gabriel wraps his arm around my shoulders. Everyone, Darcia included, is surprised I'm here tonight, with my dad still in town—and sleeping on our couch, which is a whole other level of awkward—but no way was I missing Dar's big night.

"I'm going to stay for a couple days," he'd said last night when I was going up to bed. He was standing at the foot of the stairs in jeans and a sweater and sock feet, and it was hard to remember he didn't belong here anymore, that he had ever left. "Just to give us a chance to get to know each other. But a break here and there is probably a good idea, too."

He's not wrong. I mean, I'm trying to be understanding, and I'm trying to take him being part of my life in any way as better than nothing at all, but instant family togetherness is a lot of pressure. Especially when we're all waiting for Robin's powers to misfire every other minute.

Gabriel wasn't surprised that I still wanted to come tonight, but I figured he wouldn't be. He knows how

I feel about finding Adam, not to mention Darcia's big debut. And I'm counting on him to use his special Spidey sense to get into Bay's head.

Which means I won't have to use my power at all. For the time being anyway, I'm pretty content to park that part of me in the long-term lot.

"They might not even show up," I say finally, glancing around the room. It's an addition to the original barn, with a coffee counter along one side and the stage area set up catty-corner to it. Usually the rest of the room is full of tables and a couple of thrift-store armchairs, but for events like this, rows of folding chairs are set up. I think it's supposed to give the showcases a concert atmosphere, but instead it feels a little like the high school auditorium.

It is packed, though. Four people are playing, and Dar is the second on the bill. She's so nervous, she's been jittering all day, and Thierry is here somewhere, which I bet is making it worse. I haven't seen her this moony over a boy in, like, ever.

"What exactly did you say to Bay?" Gabriel whispers. His arm is draped over the back of my chair, and the chill of the night air on it is quickly fading in the overcrowded room. "I mean, you blew him off for days."

"I said he was right." I make a hair-ball noise. "I generally groveled and said I was being stupid about what happened, and hey, why don't you meet me at this thing tonight?"

"And you think he's going to buy that?" He sounds dubious, but the lights are going down and the first performer is walking up to the stool and mike, so I just shrug and take one last look around.

I don't want to see Bay or Fiona. I don't really want them on the same planet as me, much less in the same room. But I can't forget that a kid I know might be out there somewhere, hurt or possibly dead, because he got tangled up with them.

I can't believe I let myself get tangled up with them, either, but a little guilt and a lot of shame is nothing compared to being dead.

"Oh boy," I hear Jess say when the guy at the mike starts. He's oozing emo all over the place, dyed white hair dripping into his eyes, and I can practically feel Cal falling asleep. Gabriel is rubbing his eyes, but I'd bet a week's paycheck it's just general irritation instead of a headache.

"They're only playing three songs each, right?" Gabriel mutters at the end of the second song, just as fingers snake over my knee and squeeze. I whirl to find Bay crouched beside my chair, and Fiona pressed against the wall behind him. She looks more malevolent than usual, too. Sort of like a crazy fairy who's thinking about a homicidal rampage, actually. In the low light, her eyes are glittering.

I hold a finger to my lips, even though there's nothing I want to hear less than this guy's last song, but I smile when I do it. My "so glad to see you" face is not something I pull out very often, and I elbow Gabriel at the same time.

Bay sketches a salute and straightens up to stand beside Fiona, draping himself over her the way his coat hangs on him. And then proceeds to stare just past me at Gabriel.

So totally not cool. I could swear the temperature in the room just dropped twenty degrees, and beside me Gabriel is tense, too perfectly still to be relaxed. As the song winds to an end, all I can do is cling to his hand and hope he's poking around in Bay's head. And finding something we can use in what I assume is the rest of the slimy garbage in there.

The polite applause at the end of the set is a relief, for me if not for Emo Boy. I turn around to say something to Bay in the pause before Darcia comes out, but he and Fiona are gone. I glance back at Gabriel, and he's staring at the stage like he's hypnotized.

Where the hell did they go, and how did I not hear them walking away? I twist completely around to look at the back of the room, and the big archway into the bookstore, but they're nowhere.

And Gabriel is . . . in a totally other zone. I snap my fingers and hiss his name, and he turns his head slowly toward me. Too slowly.

"Wren?"

"Did you get anything?" I whisper, leaning close. "Are you okay? Where did they go?"

He blinks, and his head swivels back to face the stage. It's so close to the careful, lifeless way that Danny moved, the hair on the back of my neck is standing up. "Darcia," he says, and smiles. Sort of.

And I am now officially freaked out.

I want to grab his hand and pull him out of the room, into the frozen night. I want to scream, and I want to find Bay, since I know he did this, whatever it is. And then later, when I have a minute, I want to pull my hair out strand by strand for thinking it was in any way a good idea to invite someone with powers like Bay's to come here, when I should have guessed he'd be getting his payback on.

And my best friend, Darcia? The one who's about to play in public for the first time? I'd kind of like to see her sing, and to stand up on my chair afterward and applaud till my hands bleed, because that's why I'm here.

She walks up to the stool, and even from here I can see her trembling. But she sits down, guitar strap over her shoulder, and pulls it onto her lap. The lighting isn't exactly professional, but it's soft and focused on her, and her hair makes a dark halo around her face.

She looks beautiful, and for a second nothing else matters.

She sings an older Ani DiFranco song first, and her fingers are so sure on the strings, I want to jump up and down and throw flowers. But as I glance across Gabriel for Jess's reaction, Gabriel's eyes stop me. Behind the flat gray is a shadow that flickers and moves as I watch, and Gabriel gasps.

Everyone's clapping as the song ends, and for a minute I freeze. It's an echo of the noise in my head, shrieking to get Gabriel out of here, desperate not to make a scene, and cheering for Darcia all at once. I grab Gabriel's hand, and his fingers tighten around mine painfully, knuckles white.

"This is the one I love," Jess leans in to whisper, beaming, as Dar starts the next song. She frowns when she sees Gabriel's face and mouths, *What's wrong?* at me. I wish I knew.

Instead of answering, I mouth back, *Tell her I'm sorry,* and stand in a crouch, tugging Gabriel after me.

He's nearly boneless, all of his strength poured into the death grip he has on my hand, and I really, really wish I hadn't thought of it as a death grip. Cal leans around Jess, confused, but she just shakes her head and points at the stage. Dar's song is already winding down.

I nearly trip over a bag someone left in the aisle, and twice Gabriel glances off the wall like a giant boy-sized bag of potatoes, but I manage to get him through the archway and into the bookstore. The girl at the counter looks up in alarm, and I paste on a completely fake smile.

"Asthma," I say, and wow, that's dumb, because he should be gasping for breath, not propped against the wall like a zombie. She just nods and goes back to her book, and for one wild second I feel like shouting, "Hey, that girl in there is going to be on the radio in a couple years, so pay attention!"

Tonight needs the biggest do-over ever.

I sling Gabriel's arm over my shoulder and steer him outside. It's frigid, the cold a vicious slap as soon as it hits, and I realize I'd been hoping it would shock the vague lifelessness out of Gabriel. Instead, he's doubling over, eyes slipping closed, and before I know it, he's huddled on the pavement, barely conscious.

It only takes me a second to decide. I pull out my cell phone and call the house, shivering as the phone rings. My mom answers, and I don't say anything but "I need Dad."

The last thing I expected to see tonight was my father with Gabriel slung over his shoulder in a fireman's carry as he climbed the stairs to the apartment. I mean, I'd envisioned Gabriel meeting my dad, probably tomorrow, totally chill, nothing big and formal and official. Instead, I had my dad laying Gabriel out on his bed, his face pinched in dread.

One day, I hope, I'm going to get something simple right the first time.

For now, I'm sitting on the edge of Gabriel's bed, holding his hand, and it feels like the only thing I do anymore. His skin looks like wet paper, a sheen of sweat on his pale forehead. His hair is plastered to his head, and he's shaking, eyes moving under his lids in staccato bursts. Olivia's still at the bar, but as soon as I work up the courage, I know I have to call her.

"I don't know, Wren. This could be a nine-one-one moment," my dad says. He's standing at the end of the bed, watching every move Gabriel makes, and I don't blame him for suggesting it. Gabriel looks stuck somewhere between a coma and a seizure, and the worst part is that it clearly hurts. Like, a lot.

"But what . . ." I get myself together, blinking back tears. "But what are they going to do if they can't find anything wrong? Bay did this, Dad, I know it."

"If this is a spell . . ." The words trail off into silence, broken only by the creak of bedsprings as Gabriel jerks in pain. "This is serious stuff, honey."

I finally look back at him, and I can see the protective dad warring with the furious father who wants to know exactly what his kid has gotten herself into. I don't have time for that, even as I fleetingly imagine what he's going to tell my mom.

Right now, I'm not sure how much time Gabriel has left.

# CHAPTER TWENTY-FOUR

"WE HAVE TO DO SOMETHING," OLIVIA SAYS. It's not quite nine on Saturday morning, and she's pacing the length of the apartment wrapped in an old sweater. She hasn't been to sleep; none of us has.

My mom comes out of Gabriel's bedroom without closing the door behind her. She's been sitting with him, doing everything she can to make him comfortable, since sometime around one this morning. I don't know what kind of spells she's used, but he's not as restless with pain anymore.

I think that's what they call "cold comfort."

Olivia is so wild with worry and rage, she's practically

vibrating. Every time she falls silent, I'm sure I can hear the echoing screams in her head. Gabriel is all she has.

I don't need anyone to remind me.

Mom brought my books when she came, leaving Robin home asleep, and Dad's been poring through them for hours.

"It's been a long time," he keeps apologizing, "and I never had to deal with anything like this before. You're sure you didn't hear him say anything? You didn't smell any herbs or notice anything strange, something he left behind?"

All I can do is shake my head and go back to the books I'm looking through. I was too freaked to think to look around, and I know I didn't hear him say anything. And even though I've seen him do magic without a word plenty of times, this is terrifying. Something like this . . . I don't even want to know what he was thinking at Gabriel to cause this.

"You're going to have to find him," Olivia announces suddenly, stopping in the middle of the room. Her arms are folded tight against her chest, and her jaw is set hard. "Find him and hold him down if you have to. But figure out what he did to my brother." She swallows back a sob and sits down suddenly on the bare floor, a puddle of sweater with a girl inside it. "And then let me at him."

My father glances up at me and nods, and when I look at Mom, she's frowning but she's not arguing. "I can keep him comfortable while your father keeps researching. I think finding this boy is probably your only choice. But I want you to go with her, Mari. Double the magic anyway."

Mari nods right before she stifles a yawn. She looks about as powerful as a kitten right now.

I lay the thick, dusty book I've been paging through on the sofa and stand up. Everything feels stiff and sore, and my head is aching with exhaustion and worry and probably hunger at this point. My Docs have been kicked under the coffee table, and as I lean down to grab them, Dad touches my back.

It's just a warm weight, no stroking or patting, but for the space of a minute I *remember* with a rush that overwhelms me. My daddy doing just that as I turned over to go to sleep, my night-light a steady gold glow on the wall, and his hand just anchoring me there in bed, a connection, a presence. I'm here, that hand said, it's okay to close your eyes.

When I straighten up, I don't try to hide the tears slipping down my cheeks, hot and fast.

Mom crosses the room and pulls me close, her hand in my hair, and her voice, gentle and steady, in my ear.

"We're going to fix this, baby. I promise you."

I manage to nod and finally stand back. My nose is dripping, and my hands are shaking, but I need to do one thing before I leave.

Gabriel is flat on his back beneath a faded West Point blanket. I took his shoes off not long after Dad and I brought him home, and his socked feet have fallen toward each other like a little kid's. I bite the inside of my cheek, hard, so I won't cry again, and lean over him, one hand on his chest. He's breathing a little easier, and he's cooler now, at least.

He hasn't opened his eyes in hours.

I lean my forehead against his. "I don't know what Bay did, but I'm going to undo it. I will. Just . . . just hold on for me, okay?"

He doesn't stir.

Aunt Mari gives me a ride to Summerhill.

It isn't until we're on campus, parked outside the dorms, that I realize I have no idea where Bay's room is. And it's not like there's a handy directory.

"Maybe I could figure out some sort of location spell," Mari says, leaning on the steering wheel and peering out the windshield at the buildings. "I've never actually done one before, but I think—"

"We don't have time to play 'Occult Nancy Drew.'" I shake my head. My hands are clenched so tight, my fingernails are digging half-moons into my palms. "Wait, I know. Jude. I can ask Jude."

"Jude?" Mari says, confused, but she's already turning the car on again. I give her the directions to Jude's apartment and sit rigid in the passenger seat as Mari takes us there.

I'm so tired, it's hard to keep my eyes open. But every time I close them, I see Gabriel's face.

Mari pulls into an empty spot on the block where Jude's apartment is, and I'm already halfway up to the door before she gets out of the car. I press buzzers until someone opens the outside door, and then I run up the stairs to Jude's apartment.

There's no answer. I keep pounding, calling for her, but the door stays firmly shut. When I press my ear to it, I don't hear anything, not that I would hear her crouching inside, ignoring me. It feels empty, but I knock one more time. "Jude, come on, I need to talk to you!"

A door down the hall opens, and a guy in a backward baseball cap and a pair of basketball shorts sticks his head out. "Christ, she's not home! Give it a frigging rest, it's, like, ass o'clock in the morning."

"It's almost ten, slacker," I snap, but I head back

downstairs, where Mari is waiting by the door.

"No luck?"

"None." I push open the door and stand on the walk, shaking. *If I can't find Jude . . .*

"Come on." Mari's hand on my back steers me toward the curb, but I glance up and down the block first. And maybe someone, somewhere, is rooting for me, because Jude is walking home with a bakery bag in one hand and a giant coffee in the other, just a block away.

My mouth falls open when she spots me—and turns around. She's not quite running, but it's close, and I lunge into a sprint to go after her. She turns the corner, and I groan.

I can hear Mari's feet pounding the sidewalk behind me even as I shout, "Jude, stop! Please, Jude! I need your help! *Jude!* I mean it, come on! He might die!"

The toe of her sneaker catches on an uneven piece of concrete in the sidewalk, and her coffee lands with a messy splash on the grass beside it, but she finally slows down. We're two blocks farther into the residential neighborhood on this side of downtown, big sprawling houses set back from the street, the bare trees arching overhead like a canopy. It's not really the kind of block where you're supposed to have messy, screaming confrontations, but I don't care.

She stops and turns around to face me as I jog toward her, panting. Mari is somewhere behind me, but I don't need her for this. I only need Jude, and suddenly I'm not at all sure what awful thing I might do if she tries to take off again.

"Who might die?" Jude says quietly when I'm finally close enough to hear her. She sets the bakery bag down on the short wall at the foot of the yard behind her. It slopes up in a graceful hill, and the wall is a perfect place to sit. I take it, still trying to catch my breath.

"Gabriel," I say simply, and let my head hang down over my chest for a minute. "Look, I know this isn't your problem, but I can't find Bay. And he . . . he did something to Gabriel last night, and I need to find him. I need to know what he did so I can fix it."

"Oh, Jesus, Wren." She drops down next to me and wipes her nose with the back of her hand. It's freezing, and her cheeks are hot pink with it.

"Look, I know what you said. But I didn't know why you said to be careful, you know?" I scrub my hands through my hair, trying to get all the facts straight so she'll understand. "I saw Bay with some other kids, and I heard them mention Adam Palicki's name. And Bay totally made the grossest moves on me and said awful things about Fiona, and that night, at the party, Gabriel got a glimpse inside Bay, and I know it was about Adam."

If I was trying to tell this sensibly, I'm not doing a very good job, but I can tell Jude is following anyway.

"But Gabriel and I, we wanted to see if . . . well, first you should know Gabriel is psychic, so we wanted to see if—"

"Wren." Jude holds a hand up, nodding. "I get it. Bay is poison. What happened to Gabriel exactly?"

"I don't know." For the first time, tears are threatening again, because at the heart of this mess is Gabriel, unconscious on his bed. "He got all spacey, and then he was in pain, and then he passed out, but he was still in pain, and he's sort of . . . comatose now, or something."

She shakes her head, closing her eyes briefly, and then stands up. "Come on. Come back to my apartment for a minute, and then I'll do whatever I can to help."

Jude tries Bay's phone when we get upstairs, and sighs when she hangs up a second later. "This number is no longer in service, apparently," she says. "I bet he just took off. I got sort of . . . freaked out about him not long ago, and probably about a week before I met you, I did a little digging on him. It seems like he's done this before. I don't think he's really a freshman, either."

"What about Fiona? Do you know her home phone

or where she lives?"

"Yup." Jude picks up her phone again, but I can tell no one's answering. "Maybe we should swing by there, just to see."

I know where we're going when we're still half a block away, and when Jude tells Mari which house to pull up to, I groan.

"Here? God." It's the house Gabriel and I were walking by when he had his first headache all those weeks ago. I can't believe it. All along, he's been picking up Bay's nasty frequency, and I had no idea.

Jude and I get out of the car and walk up the driveway. There are no cars parked there or in the garage, and the house has the locked-up, lifeless look of something empty.

"We could probably get in," Jude says with a shrug. "I mean, I know we could—it's nothing to open a door. But I don't think we're going to find anything."

"At the moment, I don't really need to add breaking and entering to my list of crimes," I tell her, and lean against the back door for a minute. "You know what happened to Adam, don't you? That's why you were so uncomfortable with them?"

She nods, her colorless hair falling forward to hide her eyes. "It was just us, Adam and Fiona and Bay and me, here. Fiona's parents were away, like always, and Bay . . .

wanted to party. Adam had been hanging around, and he didn't really have any power, but he wanted to learn the spells, the craft, and Bay liked to . . . play with him. Adam was a sweet kid." When she looks up, her eyes are glassy with tears.

"It was an accident, really. They were goofing around, and we were all drinking a little, and Adam wanted to fly. Bay had been sort of dosing him all night, giving him little jolts of magic, and I don't think Adam realized it. Next thing I knew, Bay was coming in from outside and telling us all to clean up, putting Fiona to bed. I think he did some kind of spell—she doesn't remember Adam at all now. For her, he never even existed."

I'm staring, my blood frozen into sludge inside. "Fly?"

She just nods, and suddenly I can imagine it all, Adam up on that roof right there, the blood . . .

"What did he do with the . . . the body?"

She swallows hard. "I don't know. I thought Adam had just gone home at first. But when we were leaving, I saw the . . . the blood in the driveway."

Oh God.

"I was so scared of him then, Wren." She grabs my arm, fingers too tight. "I mean, I thought it was just fun, I'd never met anyone who could do what I could do, and I knew it was sort of slimy the way he treated Fiona, but she just didn't get it, it was all a game to her, it was just make-believe, fairyland, and—"

"Stop!" I'm shaking again, my stomach rolling with the dark, foul taste of all of it. "Do your guilt on your own time, okay? Right now my boyfriend is *sick*. Can you help me or not?"

She straightens up, sniffling. "Absolutely."

There's no time for formal introductions when we get up to Olivia and Gabriel's apartment. I probably could have brought in Merlin, and Olivia would have simply nodded and told us to get out our wands.

There's no good news yet.

"I've found pieces of other spells, or spells almost like what you need, but without knowing what we're fighting, it's hard to be specific." Dad looks beyond exhausted.

"Are you a . . . what they are?" Olivia asks Jude, blunt and wild-eyed. She seems to be disappearing farther into the huge sweater every time I look at her, nothing left but crazy, knotted hair and tearstains.

Jude nods and takes off her coat and sits down next to my father. "Can I take a look? I've studied some of this, just out of curiosity."

"Kids these days," Mom says faintly, and Mari puts an arm around her.

"It was partly to get familiar with the history of the practice, and partly because . . ." Jude trails off and looks at me with a sad shrug. "Well, I was scared I might run into someone who liked the black arts."

I shudder and turn away, wrapping my arms around myself. The door to Gabriel's bedroom is still partway open, and I walk over to it to peek inside.

It doesn't look like he's moved. For a moment, he looks so much like Danny did, lying on the same bed just months ago, dead and undead and hurting all because of me, that my stomach turns with horror.

But the feeling twists itself into something new a moment later: determination. No way am I losing Gabriel. Absolutely not.

"Give me a book," I say, facing the others again. "I'm figuring this out right now."

# CHAPTER TWENTY-FIVE

THREE HOURS LATER, I'M AS READY AS I'M ever going to be. The words in the books are running together, and every new suggestion is just confusing the issue. Dad keeps muttering about "what this kid did to Gabriel" and every time he says, "this kid," his voice drops into a growl. Mom and Mari are propping up each other in exhaustion, and Olivia is passed out on the couch. Jude's flipping through the books so intensely, she barely says a word, scribbling notes on a pad beside her instead.

I'm done. I'm getting my boyfriend back *now*.

I raised Danny from the grave without a book, after

all, even if I did crib some notes. I can heal Gabriel, too.

"Okay," I say, standing up, and it's so quiet in the room that everyone jumps. Even Olivia stirs on the sofa, and Mari goes over to get her up.

"Honey, did you find something?" Mom asks. She's rubbing her eyes.

"Sort of." I attempt a smile. "I'm just using basic principles here, but I think it will work with enough, well, power behind it."

Dad looks stricken and even afraid. I don't have time to deal with how awful that makes me feel for him, though. "You know I can't . . ."

"I know, it's okay." I nod at him, and Jude closes her book and looks up at me, hands folded.

"Basic principles" are just that, and I don't want to admit that some of them I borrowed from *Buffy* and *Charmed*. But I explain that we'll need a circle, and they'll have to repeat the words I give them three times.

Not to mention the full force of everyone's power hurled at Gabriel like magical grenades. Peaceful, healing magical grenades anyway.

"It could work," Mari says, and Olivia murmurs, "It has to work."

"I wish Mom was here," my mother says, finally looking up at my dad. Her smile is rueful, brief, and she reaches across the table to squeeze his hand just as quickly. "Thank you, Sam."

He shakes his head. "Least I can do. Literally." He touches my shoulder as he passes, and I lean into it for a second, letting the warmth bleed in. "I'm going to see what Robin's up to. I'm . . . I'm so sorry I can't do more, kiddo."

Gratitude wells up like blood from a wound, hot and urgent. "Daddy, you've . . . you've done a lot. Thank you." I take a minute to hug him hard, drinking in the solid comfort of him. It's beginning to feel familiar again.

"Now? Please?" Olivia's voice is a husk of sound as she waits at the doorway to Gabriel's room. Dad watches as the five of us walk inside, but I hear the door to the apartment open and close as we gather two on each side of Gabriel's bed and me at the foot. He's still lost somewhere, drifting, anchored here by nothing but his body.

It's up to us now.

"You know I don't . . . have abilities, right?" Olivia whispers to me.

"Intentions matter more than magic," Jude tells her with a smile, and Olivia relaxes.

"I have to get a few things," I tell them. "For now, just stand here in a circle, and think the best, most healing thoughts you can at him. If you pray, go ahead. It won't hurt."

Mom's expression is pinched with concern, but she nods, and all four of them close their eyes, hands clasped. The simple gesture is so powerful, I have to choke back tears.

I find a candle in the kitchen, and Olivia's been growing lavender on the kitchen windowsill for a few months. It's not much, but it's supposed to be good for love and healing. I take a bowl down from the cabinet and gently strip leaves and petals into the bottom of the bowl. I don't have my athame, but a kitchen knife will probably do just as well. I scrub it clean with steaming-hot water and soap and carry all of it into the other room.

The hush is calming, so I walk softly to the end of the bed and place the bowl on the mattress between Gabriel's feet. I put the candle on the dresser and light it with a pack of matches I found in the kitchen drawer, and turn around to face the others.

"Okay, this is not the best idea, but I think it will help. If you don't want to do this part, you don't have to." I hold up the knife a little sheepishly. "Just a drop from your fingertip will do it, I think."

"Oh, Wren," Mom says, but she disappears for a

moment and comes back with a wet paper towel. "Wipe it in between. Well."

I make the first prick and hand the knife to Olivia. It doesn't take much to squeeze a fat drop from my finger, and it darkens the lavender when it falls. The others follow without a word, and when I've put the knife away everyone joins hands again.

"Repeat the last part after me three times, okay?" I tell them, and take one last look at Gabriel, pale and motionless, before I close my eyes to begin.

*Please, please let this work.*

My voice shakes with the first words.

*We call upon greater powers to heal this boy*
*For him we seek peace and health*
*His life was cursed, to heal him is our plea*

*Spirits bright, spirits kind*
*Brigid, Airmid, Dian Cécht*
*All the hooded spirits*
*Witness our invocation*

*To health you return, Gabriel*
*Peace awaits you*
*A curse has no hold on you anymore*

*By the light of the sun*
*By the light of our love*
*We command this to be*

*With this symbol of Gabriel*
*With our blood*
*We command this to be*

*Heal him, great spirits*
*Heal him, powers kind*
*Heal him, great spirits*
*Heal him, powers good*

Four voices join me as I repeat the last verse, echoing twice more—Mom's soft and steady, Jude's determined, Olivia's breaking with tears. Mari's voice is strong and sweet, completely confident, and I want to hug her.

I take a deep breath before I open my eyes, and we're all frozen, hands clasped tight, staring at Gabriel with dread and hope and love. The silence rings all around us, complete and stark, and then Gabriel gasps.

Olivia's grip tightens so hard, I wince, and Jude steps back from the bed, hand to her mouth. Mom and Mari are still frozen, waiting.

And me? I'm pushing them out of the way to lean

over him, shaking so hard I can barely see. "Gabriel?"

He draws another long, shuddering breath, and opens his eyes. They're fogged, unfocused, but in another moment they're clear, narrowing and blinking and the eyes I love.

I'm the first thing he sees. And his slow, sleepy smile is all I need.

# CHAPTER TWENTY-SIX

"SO WHAT HAPPENED?" JESS BLOWS ON HER latte so hard the whipped cream ripples. "Is he okay now?"

"It's migraines, I guess," I tell her, but I'm staring into my own coffee. Geoff made it special for me, and there's a bag of pastries and cookies in the back to take to Gabriel and Olivia when I leave. Gabriel has grown on him, and even Trevor thinks, and I quote, that Olivia is "adorable enough to eat."

"I'm so sorry we missed the last song," I say to Darcia, who's nibbling her way through a ginger-cranberry muffin with brown-butter-cinnamon glaze. Or something. I hate it when Geoff makes things that take longer to say than to eat. "You were awesome, though."

Dar actually smirks. She licks a shiny smear of sugar off her finger, and says, "Well, next time, hopefully you won't have to miss it."

Jess lifts a brow. "Next time?"

Dar bites her bottom lip, but her grin escapes anyway. "They asked me back. Next month."

"No way!" I high-five her across the table, and Jess leans over to plant a noisy kiss on her cheek. "Rock star all the way. I told you."

"I don't know about rock star," Dar protests, but she's still beaming when she bites into her muffin again.

"I'll do all the promotion." Jess is gazing out the window, mouth pursed as she plans. "Email blasts, Facebook, free MP3s. Wren, you can be the tour photographer."

Dar and I both laugh, but I like the idea. After everything that's happened, it won't be a huge deal if it's too late to join yearbook, but I'm still going to try. What stings is that I came so close to believing magic was the only thing that made me special.

I shake off the thought of Bay and pick up my coffee. "I have to go in a minute. I told Gabriel I'd come over now that he's not, you know, writhing in pain."

Jess snorts a laugh, and I manage a smile, because there's nothing else to say. Migraines never killed anyone, as far as I know. But what happened to Gabriel was close.

"Hey," Dar says, touching my hand. "He is okay, right?"

I straighten up, trying not to shiver. "He is. And I should probably take him the instant sugar high Geoff provided."

"Call later," Jess says as I get up from the table, and my smile is wider this time. These are my friends, and I don't need anyone different. We're all pretty perfect just the way we are.

It's still cold as I walk to Gabriel's, blue and clear, and I'm surprised to find him sitting on the front steps. He's bundled into his heaviest jacket, and a gray wool scarf is looped around his neck. He stands up when he sees me.

"What are you doing out here?" I ask him, stretching up to kiss him. His lips are chilly and smooth.

"I had to escape," he says, and takes the café bag to peek inside. "My sister is in full hover mode. I think she has a future as a spacecraft."

I elbow him as we sit down on the steps together, and he pulls one of my feet toward his, lining them up side by side. He's wearing the blue sneakers from the pictures, and I'm in my Docs, as usual. I lean my head on his shoulder and reach for his hand, tangling our fingers together.

"So that happened," Gabriel finally says, and I have to laugh even as I elbow him again. "What?"

I don't want to ruin this moment. I don't want to ruin anything again, ever, especially not between the two of us. But the last few days have washed over me like a wave, rinsing so much clean, and I feel lighter than I have in a long time.

Until I think about Gabriel.

"It's your turn, you know," I say after thinking about the words carefully.

"My turn to . . . cast an evil spell on someone?" He makes a face, but he's smiling.

"To spill, Gabriel." I stand up so I can face him, but it's hard not to pace back and forth on the walk. "I can't even explain what it was like when you were lying in that bed, in so much pain. I haven't been that scared in . . . Well, you know the last time I was that scared."

His brows touch, furrowing into the beginning of a frown, but he doesn't look away.

"I can't lose you, Gabriel. I love you." I shrug and let the words hang there, simple and honest, completely unadorned. "But I keep wondering who it is I love. There are so many things I know about you, but they all have to do with, well, me. That you would never hurt me, that you want me to be happy, that you want me to be safe. It's beginning to feel like I made you up, you know? The perfect boyfriend, who's always there, who gives me the most awesome gifts ever, who takes a frigging magical *bullet* for me. But it's like . . . it's like looking in a mirror or something. I can take care of myself, you know? What I want is . . ." I trail off, sighing. "I want to know *you*, Gabriel. The way you know me."

He unfolds himself from the steps, long and lean and so quiet I want to shake him. Instead, I wait while he walks toward me, offering a hand. "Let's walk, huh?"

"Are you sure you're up to it?"

"I feel fine." He squeezes my hand. "No magic hangover at all."

I'm not sure this was true yesterday, because he woke up groggy and disoriented, and it took a few hours of nodding in and out of painless sleep for him to totally be himself again. But I'm not going to argue.

"It's, you know, hard to talk about this stuff," Gabriel says when we're halfway down the block.

"What stuff?"

He groans. "If I could just barf it out, it wouldn't be hard."

"No barfing." I bump his hip with mine. "What's the

hardest part? Start there maybe? Get it over with?"

He stops suddenly, and I stumble against him, startled. But when I see the look on his face, I let the snark on my tongue dissolve. "It's nothing really horrible. Me, I mean. I didn't kill a man in Vegas, and I'm not, like, an alien, and my sister isn't secretly in hiding from the mob or something. It's just . . ." He swallows hard. "It's just my dad."

I take both of his hands in mine. "We all have them, you know, one way or another. You can *tell* me, Gabriel."

An elderly woman is coming up the sidewalk with a beagle that looks just as old, and we move to one side so she can pass. Gabriel watches her go and finally looks down at me again.

"It's just . . . it's nothing to be proud of. Your dad, even though he left, he never wanted to hurt you, you know? That's why he left. To keep all of you safe."

I know he's trying, and for a moment the world rocks to a halt. We're balanced over something deep, something dark, and all I can do is hold on as we fall.

"I know my story, Gabriel," I say when he's silent for too long. "Tell me yours."

He lets go of my hands and starts walking again. He's running from something, even if it's just telling me, but I catch up and grab his arm. I'm startled to find he's already talking. ". . . in prison now, in Ohio. He's a con man, Wren. It's the only job he's ever had, really. I think my mom thought he was . . . something else. Maybe I just want to believe that, I don't know."

I can't say anything yet. I have to let him tell it all, the way he wants to. But I tuck my hand into his jacket pocket as we walk.

"He used her, all the time." His eyes skid sideways, judging my reaction, and I just nod. "He used her gift to scam people. And then she got sick. So he used me instead."

Horror uncoils in my stomach, raw and sharp. But he's not done yet.

"And after my mom died, he dragged us all over. Long cons took a while, so sometimes we'd get to stay somewhere for a few months, but we could never really make friends. And half the time we were living in some trailer or some shithole apartment I wouldn't have wanted anyone to see."

It's scary, how dead his voice sounds, how cold and flat. Maybe if he makes it sound like just another thing that happened, a simple fact, it doesn't hurt as much.

"He's hurt people, Wren." When he looks at me this time, I can see the shame of it in his eyes. "I just . . . We're done with him, me and Olivia. But he'll be out one day. And I never want him to find us, or you. I never . . . I never wanted to have to tell you what I come from."

"But it's not your fault!" I throw my arms around him, squeezing tight. "You have to know that. You and Olivia, you're good people, Gabriel. Whatever your father did, that's on him. Seriously."

He doesn't seem convinced. "But . . . I come from that."

"So what?" I step back, throwing my hands in the air. "So. What. It's not a disease, Gabriel. Your father made choices and so did you. You and Olivia, you chose to come here, to start over, to leave him behind. Every day, you're not living the life your father did. How can you not see that?"

He stares at me, and that dark, deep place closes up in the space of one breath. After a moment, something like a smile tugs at one corner of his mouth. "So you're saying I'm, like, a total moron."

"Pretty much." I kick the toe of one sneaker with my boot, gently. "My boyfriend, the giant dumbass."

He actually laughs. "You could make a T-shirt. 'I'm with Dumbass.'"

"I think I will." I grab his hand and turn us around so we're headed back toward his apartment. After a second,

I pull him closer and glance up at him. "Thank you. For telling me that."

He shrugs, dorky cute when he's sheepish. "I'm sorry I didn't do it before."

We walk in silence for a little while, but it's comfortable, familiar. It's nice, until I realize my own words are echoing in my head: *"Every day, you're not living the life your father did."*

And neither am I. For the first time since Gabriel told me what he'd sensed about my dad, I'm not worried about using my power. I've never used magic the way he did, and I don't want to. I want to explore it, because it is part of me, and it's pretty cool when it comes right down to it. But I know I have to respect it, too. And that doesn't seem like a burden.

I feel so light, I think with one breath and a little focus I could float up over the rooftops and into the trees. Maybe even take Gabriel with me. And inside me, my magic is still wide-open sky. I know I can fly when I want to.

I tug Gabriel's hand to get him to stop, and step backward. "How good do you feel?"

"I told you, I feel fine!" He rolls his eyes. "Wow, now I know what I must sound like."

"Fine, huh?" I grin, and turn him so his back is to me.

Then I push him into a crouch and climb on. "You are fine," I whisper in his ear when he's standing up and not laughing anymore. "Take me up to your place and show me how fine, huh?"

I'm pretty sure he's blushing as he heads toward home.

# EPILOGUE

THE MEMORIAL SERVICE FOR ADAM IS HELD the first week in February, at Saint Francis. Gabriel and I are a little late, so we end up standing in the back, straining to hear the priest. Audrey is way up front, sitting right behind Adam's family. She's going to speak, too.

Gabriel and I decided to call the police anonymously about Adam. Afterward, I know they searched Fiona's house and property, and they were looking for Bay, but nothing ever turned up. Fiona was already eighteen, so there was nothing they could do about her, even when she never came home. Jude told me they'd interviewed all kinds of kids on campus, and once they knew about

Bay and Fiona's relationship, the police were willing to bet she'd left with him of her own free will.

I wasn't so sure.

I see Jude sometimes now. We're not friends exactly, but she's someone I can talk to about my power, someone who isn't related to me, anyway. She's a really good artist, and I think someday I'm going to show her some of Danny's pieces.

More than that, I think I'll probably tell her about Danny at some point. The whole story. She has a lot of guilt about Adam, even if his death wasn't really her fault. Maybe if I share what I've done, she'll feel a little better.

I hate that the police never found Adam's body. But the fact that they had a lead and something of an idea about what happened to him helped his family out a little bit. The memorial service is proof of that. It's a way to say good-bye, after all.

I'd said good-bye to my dad the same Sunday when Gabriel and I talked. He had to get back to work, but he made it clear that talking on the phone and sending email was something he wanted from now on. I was glad, too. I just hoped the next time he visited, we would be a little lower on magical emergencies.

Robin had a hard time with him leaving, doing the whole Velcro hug thing until I was worried Dad wasn't actually breathing anymore. Mom had already said her good-byes and was upstairs in her room with Mari, and I couldn't imagine how hard it was for her. To love someone like that and know you can't be together? Love is so huge and so sweet when you find it, I'll never understand how it manages to turn around and smack you so often.

I walked Dad out to his car, and he paused before he got in. "Just . . . be careful," he said.

"I will, Dad." I hugged him then, too, breathing in that familiar leather-and-soap scent as long as I could. "But I don't think you need to worry."

He scoffed, barking out a laugh. "Uh, I'm a parent, kiddo. That's what I'm going to do anyway."

I glance at Gabriel now, watching his face as he listens to the priest. Gabriel didn't have that, except from his mom, and she was taken way too soon. It's not fair. In my secret fantasies, Gabriel's father and Bay run into each other somewhere, and the only words I have for that scenario are "cage match."

"Audrey's going to speak now," Gabriel whispers, glancing down at the program. "That's going to be hard."

I tuck my arm in his and lay my head on his shoulder. It will be hard. But whatever it is, I'm pretty sure now that Gabriel and I will always get through it.

# ACKNOWLEDGMENTS

MANY THANKS TO THE PEOPLE WHO HELD MY hand as I wrote this book: Stephen, as always, who propped me up a lot of the time; my parents, who have always believed and are always willing to lend a hand; Lee, who literally kept me going in more ways than I can count and loves me even when I forget to send her cupcakes; ita, who patiently listened to me whine every day; my wonderful agent, Maureen Walters, who is always right there cheering; and the fantastic people at HarperTeen, foremost the ever-supportive Erica Sussman. I'm lucky she still likes me. Last, so much love to my kids, who are incredibly patient with me, and always have a hug ready.

# BE CAREFUL
## WHAT YOU WISH FOR.

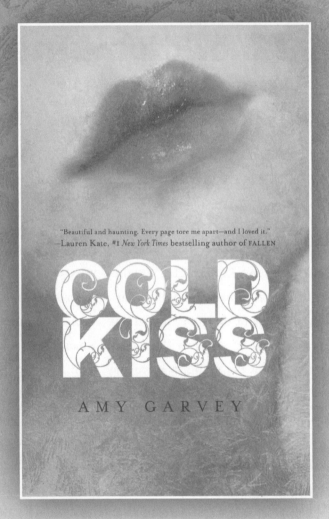

"Beautiful and haunting. Every page tore me apart—and I loved it."
—Lauren Kate, #1 *New York Times* bestselling author of FALLEN

# COLD KISS

AMY GARVEY

Discover the devastating choice that started it all.